DeWitt's Strike

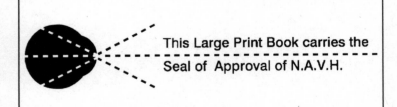

This Large Print Book carries the
Seal of Approval of N.A.V.H.

A RIDGE PARKMAN WESTERN

DeWITT'S STRIKE

GREG HUNT

THORNDIKE PRESS
A part of Gale, Cengage Learning

Farmington Hills, Mich • San Francisco • New York • Waterville, Maine
Meriden, Conn • Mason, Ohio • Chicago

GALE
CENGAGE Learning®

LIBRARY OF CONGRESS CATALOGING-IN-PUBLICATION DATA

Names: Hunt, Greg, 1947– author.
Title: Dewitt's strike : a Ridge Parkman western / by Greg Hunt.
Description: Large print edition. | Waterville, Maine : Thorndike Press, 2016. |
    Series: Thorndike press large print western
Identifiers: LCCN 2016023581 | ISBN 9781410489661 (hardcover) | ISBN 1410489663
    (hardcover)
Subjects: LCSH: Large type books. | GSAFD: Western stories.
Classification: LCC PS3558.U46768 D49 2016 | DDC 813/.54—dc23
LC record available at https://lccn.loc.gov/2016023581

Published in 2016 by arrangement with Greg Hunt

Printed in Mexico
1 2 3 4 5 6 7 20 19 18 17 16

DeWitt's Strike

CHAPTER 1

Soon after he rode down below the tree line and started working his way through the maze of forested draws, switchbacks, and dead ends, Ridge Parkman shed his heavy wool coat, rolling it in a tight bundle and tying it on the back of his saddle along with his bedroll and meager store of remaining provisions. It had seemed odd to wear such heavy clothing in July, but the nighttime temperatures in the high country often dropped below freezing even in the middle of summer, and sometimes the harsh, wet winds could be brutal.

He had never been in this part of Colorado before and had only a vague idea where he was, but he knew he must be nearing his destination. He had ridden according to the directions he received in the infrequent settlements along the way, and the country generally lay about as he had been told it would.

It had been a tough two-week ride across the Rocky Mountains from Denver. Even for travelers merely wanting to cross the mountains on their way to the West Coast there were no easy routes to reach the western side of the range. But for a man headed for one remote mining settlement far off the established routes and trails, the going could get downright treacherous. Besides the natural barriers that the terrain put in a man's way, there were many dangers caused by man that were far worse than anything nature could devise.

The army called this area pacified. After several major campaigns against bands of Sioux, Cheyenne, Arapahoe, and Apache, they had declared the hostiles conquered. But they had failed to get word to all the small wandering bands of Indians who roamed this territory to tell them that they were whipped, and any white man who valued his life and his scalp had to keep a sharp eye out to keep ownership of them. The rugged mountains were also a natural haven for the wildest collection of bandits, back-shooters, renegades, and runaways in the country.

Sure, the area was peaceful enough, but only as long as one man didn't come in close contact with another. When that happened, the peace often ended suddenly.

But Parkman had made it across this time. That was something. And now he knew De-Witt's Strike must be somewhere close by, at least if he could trust the random maps scratched in the dust outside cabin doorways or sketched on hunks of tree bark by men who said they knew what they were talking about.

He was working his way down a narrow ravine, taking it slow and letting his horse choose the pathway at his own speed. At one point the ravine widened out into a grassy meadow about fifty yards wide and two hundred yards long. There he paused and dismounted to let his horse drink from the clear, cold brook that rushed along beside the trail. Ridge kneeled down beside the brook and brought a handful of the frigid water up to his mouth. He drank his fill and then refilled his half-empty canteen.

He had ridden on past midday and now his stomach was growling with hunger, but he decided to wait until evening to eat. Only one can of beans and a dozen hardtack biscuits remained from the stores he had brought along with him from Denver. He had supplemented his diet along the way with fresh meat killed along the trail and he thought that if he pitched his camp early in the evening, he might have time to scout around and stir up some game to cook with the beans.

Before mounting up, he took a couple of the biscuits from his saddlebags, putting one in his shirt pocket and holding the other in his teeth as he stepped back up into the saddle. They would take the edge off his hunger until he stopped again.

President Grant, normally a calm, unexcitable horse, danced around nervously as Ridge settled into the saddle. The movement puzzled Ridge and he looked cautiously up and down the trail for any unexpected intruder such as a man or a bear that could have spooked the horse. But he saw nothing.

Then came the faint sound of crackling gunfire, borne on the wind like the echoes of a long-forgotten battle. Down in a ravine like he was, it was hard to tell what direction the sound was coming from, but he guessed it was somewhere southwest of him, in the approximate direction he was now riding.

He turned President Grant downhill, riding cautiously now and watching the trail ahead closely. With bullets flying in the neighborhood, anybody he met on the trail would likely start blasting before they

10

thought to ask if he was friend or foe. He was not anxious for a fight, but neither was he willing to be dropped from the saddle before he could proclaim his neutrality.

A few hundred yards on down the mountainside the ravine opened out onto a thick jumble of boulders on the steep side of a valley. Ridge stopped his horse there and stepped to the ground. Carrying his old long-barreled Sharps .50 buffalo rifle and his spyglass, he scrambled up the side of one of the largest boulders and surveyed the scene below him.

At first it was hard to tell what was going on down there, except that a bunch of men were scattered around behind rocks and bushes shooting at each other. When he brought the spyglass up to his eye, he began to get a clearer picture of the battle. Apparently seven or eight men had two or three others pinned down under a wagon beside a clump of boulders and were trying to kill them. Most of the attackers were too far away and too well concealed for him to spot, but he could get an idea of their number by the puffs of smoke when they fired their weapons. Two or three men nearer to him were in view as tiny stick figures crouching near the ground and raising up occasionally to shoot.

Ridge's good sense told him that it was not the smartest thing in the world to meddle in somebody else's fight. He knew good men who had been hurt or killed when they stuck their noses in another man's troubles and could not get them out again. But all that logical thinking did no good. He knew he could not just sit up there and watch as the men at the wagon were killed.

He laid the big, clumsy Sharps .50 down beside him and quickly loaded it with one of the husky, bottle-shaped rounds. It was a nuisance to carry this second rifle on a long ride on horseback, but in situations such as this it earned its keep. A bullet from his shorter Winchester .44 carbine would never travel far enough to reach those men down there, but the Sharps could handle the job.

He located one of the attackers in the sights of the gun, then drew a bead on a boulder a couple of feet to one side of him. That should let him know, Ridge thought, that he'd likely get his backsides dusted if he didn't pull, his stakes and hightail it.

The roar of the weapon rolled out over the valley like a cannon shot and the thumb-sized bullet went singing away on its mission. "Damn, I'd hate to hear one of those rascals screamin' toward me," Ridge mumbled as he laid the rifle down to reload.

But his shot did not have the desired effect. The man down below turned and started uselessly firing his rifle in Ridge's direction. "You're either a fool or you don't know much about guns, mister," Ridge mumbled as he raised the rifle for another shot. The second bullet knocked the man off his feet and left him thrashing around on the ground, grabbing at his lower leg.

But the others continued their attack on the men under the wagon, and one or two were getting dangerously close. Ridge quickly reloaded and looked for another target. He aimed at a man who was easing around to a position where he would be behind the pinned-down men. It took two shots before Ridge hit his target, but after the second shot the man whirled and dropped facedown in the dirt.

That seemed to do it. One by one the attacking men began to fall back, still firing repeatedly as they worked their way to where their horses were hidden in a grove of trees. Ridge reloaded the rifle and then watched until the attackers mounted up and disappeared toward the head of the valley.

For a few more minutes there was no movement at the wagon. Finally one man crept cautiously out from under it and looked around, first up and down the valley and then up toward where Ridge was. Ridge stood up on the boulder and waved to let the man know where he was. Then he slid down off the rock and returned to President Grant. It took him several minutes to ride down through the rocks to the bullet-riddled wagon in the valley basin.

He found only two men there, one standing beside the wagon and the other lying under it, either dead or wounded. The young man who stood covering Ridge with a rifle had the cold gaze of a man who had learned to trust nobody in this wild western country. His face was darkly tanned and beginning to wrinkle from constant exposure to the sun and the weather, and his clothes were filthy and ragged. The other man who lay under the wagon appeared to be much older, but it was hard for Ridge to tell much about his features because his face and shaggy beard were covered with dirt and blood.

Miners, Ridge thought, probably headed into town to cash in their earnings when the bushwhackers found them.

"Your pardner dead?" Ridge asked as he carefully dismounted. While trying to appear casual, he glanced around the area to see if he could spot some third man covering him from a hidden location.

"I don't know," the man with the rifle said without emotion. "I ain't had time to check him. Things been happenin' too fast."

"Wal, we can check him now," Ridge said. "While I was up there on that rock I watched them fellers ride plumb off. I think they decided they didn't want to tangle with this buffalo gun no more."

"Can't say I blame 'em," the man said. "Every time you fired that thing, it sounded like somebody was tryin' to blow the side of the mountain up."

Ridge got his canteen off his saddle and went over to the downed man. He pulled him partly out from under the wagon and took a close look at the wound. It started at the left temple and skimmed back above his ear. Though it appeared to be nothing more than a deep crease, it was bleeding profusely. Ridge took off his bandanna, rinsed it in the water from the canteen, and swabbed gingerly at the wound. As he worked, he looked up, exasperated at the young man who was still covering him with the rifle.

"You can point that thing at me all day if you want to, mister," Ridge said, "but if I'd wanted to drop you, I'd have done it while I was still up there on that rock. Now why don't you put the rifle down an' help me with your friend here before he bleeds to death."

The young man considered it a moment, then reluctantly leaned the rifle against the wagon. As he knelt beside Ridge, he asked, "What do you want me to do?"

"I don't guess you've got any medicine or bandages, do you?"

"Nope."

"Nor any whiskey?"

"No whiskey either."

"The best we can do is get him cleaned up an' bandaged, then. Maybe it won't fester. I've got a clean shirt in my saddlebags. We can tear that up for bandages, I guess. Go get it."

As Ridge began to work on the wound, cleaning the dirt and grit out of it, the old man began to show signs of life. When he became fully conscious he started thrashing around, but Ridge pinned him to the ground until he calmed down.

"It's okay, Abe," the younger man said as he came back with the shirt. "You got shot an' this man's tryin' to take care of you."

"Feels like he's tryin' to rip the skin off the side of my head," Abe complained sourly. "Who in hell are you, anyway?"

"He took our side 'gainst them raiders an' helped run 'em off."

"So's he could come down here 'an have the pleasure of scalpin' me all by hisself," Abe accused.

"Look, you old coot," Ridge said sternly but without anger. "You can lay here jawin' while you bleed to death out the side of your head, or you can let me clean this gash an' bandage it. It don't make me no nevermind either way."

"Wal, jus' take it easy, boy," Abe said, calming down and allowing Ridge to tend the wound. "Can't you see I'm an old man?"

Ridge dashed the last of the water on the deep injury and began tearing the shirt into long, wide strips.

"Dolf, where's the Injun?" Abe asked. "Did they get 'im?"

"He's out there somewhere," Dolf said. "Right after they got you, he went crawlin' out through the brush with that big knife in his hand. He'll be back."

It took Ridge a few minutes to get the wound bandaged. When he finished, the old man got to his feet, but he was still weak and a little shaky from the loss of blood.

"I reckon we're obliged to you," he told Ridge. "Them skunks had us cold. My name's Abe Lovett, an' this ornery Dutchman here's Adolph Rieger."

"Ridge Parkman. Glad to know you,"

Ridge said, shaking their hands. "Gen'rally I try to stay out of other men's fights when I can help it, but it looked like they had you in shore 'nough tight down here. Who were they, anyway?"

"Jes' raiders is all we know," Abe said. "These hills is crawlin' with some of the lowdownest, belly crawlin'est, backshootin'est frontier trash you ever saw. This is gold country."

"Yeh, I heard tell 'bout a big strike some-where round here. You men miners?"

"Right now we're jus' tryin' to be," Abe said. "We got us a claim up north of here, but so far we've only dug out beans an' bacon money. There's gold there, though. I kin feel it. We jes' ain't dug deep 'nough into that dad blamed mountain yet."

"That's our own personal affairs," Dolf told Abe curtly. "You don't need to go bab-blin' it to every stranger that comes ridin' along."

Ridge gave the young man a curious glance.

"See what I mean 'bout him bein' or-nery?" Abe complained to Ridge. "I swear it's a blamed chore to get along with him sometimes. You reckon all them Dutchmen over in that place them people live is as snippety all the time as this one is?"

18

"I was a quiet, even-tempered man 'til I hooked up with you, you greasy ol' bear skinner," Dolf snapped.

Ridge recognized the earmarks of a long-standing, amiable feud. Such never-ending arguments sometimes helped pass the time for lonely, isolated men such as these.

The Indian's approach to the wagon was so silent that one moment he was not there, and a minute later when Ridge looked around, there he was. He was a tall, handsome man with thick, shoulder-length black hair and an intense, unreadable gaze. He wore dirty, ill-fitting white man's clothing, but on his feet he wore soft, light moccasins instead of boots. In his right hand he carried a ten-inch sheath knife.

"That there's Oak," Abe said. "His real name's Okabittie or something, but we can't say it so we jes' call him Oak. He's our third pardner. Oak, this here's Ridge Parkman."

"My name is Okkibettebah of the Cherokee Nation," the Indian said. "And you are the one who shot from the rocks above. Thank you for helping."

"Did you find any of them, Oak?" Dolf asked.

"One is dead up there from his rifle," Oak said, indicating the hillside above them, "and in another place there was much

blood, but no man. One more died, too."
He stuck the knife in his belt sheath significantly.

"Kilt two an' wounded one. That ain't bad," Abe said. "An' all we got out of it was jes' one little scratch."

"Yeh, but we'd best pack it up an' get out of here before they decide to come back an' change the tally," Dolf said.

"Yeh, they must think we got somethin' worth takin'," Abe said. "I bet they wouldn't bother with us if they knew we didn't have but a thimbleful of gold dust to show for the last two months' work."

"What about the dead men?" Ridge asked.

"Let the buzzards have 'em," Dolf said bitterly.

"Personally, I don't believe in it," Ridge said. "I'd dig a hole an' plant my worst enemy 'fore I'd let him lay out in the sun for wolf bait — least when there's time for buryin'."

"He's right, Dolf," Abe said. "We can haul 'em into town an' bury 'em in the boot hill there. Maybe it'll give somebody the idee that we're a little bit tougher'n we look to be."

Ridge and the Indian carried the bodies of the two dead outlaws to the wagon and covered them with a piece of canvas. Then the group was ready to go into DeWitt's Strike. They followed a trail which wound its way raggedly down the middle of the valley. Despite his wound, Abe took the reins of the wagon and Dolf and Oak rode in back, keeping a vigil with their rifles ready.

Ridge rode on ahead and scouted the trail for a while, then dropped back and rode alongside the wagon. "How far is it on into DeWitt's Strike?" he asked Abe.

" 'Bout four or five more miles," the old man told him. "We was headin' in 'cause we got word the supply wagons got back from Adobe City. We brung along all our stake 'cause we need everythin' up at the mine — dynamite an' fuse, tools, nails, meat, beans, flour. . . . Can't afford much with the dust we got from pannin' but we'll buy 'nough to get by."

Shortly before they reached the edge of town, Abe stopped the wagon and the men took a few minutes to bathe and wash their clothes in the clear, cold water of the stream that flowed down the middle of the valley.

CHAPTER 2

Nobody paid much attention when the four men, one on horseback and three in a wagon, came into town. There was not even much interest shown when the wagon pulled up in front of the carpenter's shop and the canvas cover was removed from the two bodies in back. No more than half a dozen men paused to watch as the corpses were unloaded. The bodies of dead men were no unusual sight here.

Ridge helped Dolf and Oak carry the bodies into the back of the shop, and though there was no local lawman to question the killings, he explained to the carpenter and a few other bystanders that the dead men were would-be robbers. As Ridge talked, the carpenter was rifling through the pockets of the dead men with practiced ease. His search produced a couple of gold coins and some other change, and he seemed satisfied that it was enough to pay for wood coffins and grave digging for the two.

Outside the shop, Ridge parted company with the three miners, promising to meet them later for supper. They were headed to the freight office to cash in their gold dust and buy supplies, but Ridge had a slug of whiskey on his mind. Leading his horse, he started down the wide, muddy main street of the town.

DeWitt's Strike was much the same as countless other ragtag tent towns that sprang up wherever gold and silver discoveries were made. It had grown up haphazardly on one side of the crossing of the small river that flowed down the middle of the wide valley. The hills and mountain slopes on both sides of the town were pocked with the diggings of prospectors and the gaping mouths of a few producing mines. Other mines and sluicing operations were scattered for miles up and down the valley.

In its first few months of existence DeWitt's Strike had become a bustling little town with nearly seven hundred inhabitants, but it still contained only a handful of wooden buildings, including the shipping station, several saloons, a couple of restaurants, and the carpenter's shop. The shipping company owner lived in the only wood frame house in town.

It was a wide-open little settlement with no town government and no semblance of law and order. There were frequent fights, shootings, robberies, and murders, and what passed locally for justice generally came from impromptu citizens' juries whose verdict was almost invariably death by hanging. Parkman had been in places like this before and he knew that here in DeWitt's Strike it would be no trouble at all for a man to find all sorts of ways to get himself killed.

He paused in the street outside the Last Nuggett Saloon, considering whether to stop there for his drink. The wood frame building sported a painting of a scantily clad maiden sprawled across its high wooden false front, as well as numerous signs proclaiming the prices of drinks and the types of gambling available inside.

Through the open door Ridge could see the drinkers and hell raisers jammed in shoulder to shoulder, and the din pouring out into the street was just one level below that of a full-fledged riot. As he watched, the crowd near the door parted slightly and a body, propelled by unseen hands, came hurtling into the street. The rubber-limbed drunk landed face down in a mud puddle near the hitching rail. He raised up weakly onto one elbow, looked around like a man waking up in another world, rolled over onto his back, and passed out. Ridge tugged on President Grant's reins and started on down the street.

He stopped at last and hitched his horse in front of another saloon further on down the street near the edge of town. This place was housed in an enclosure of canvas tied over a wooden frame. It was only half as full as the other saloon, with perhaps fifty men standing along the plank bar or seated at the twenty or so tables around the room. It was an ordinary crowd of miners, gamblers, con men, thieves, rogues, and fortune hunters.

Standing at the door a moment, Ridge glanced around briefly to see if anybody seemed on the prod. Fights broke out like bolts of lightning in this sort of place and he did not want to walk into the middle of a pack of senseless trouble. But the place seemed quiet enough at the moment and nobody paid him the slightest attention. He walked over to the bar and held up one finger to the bartender.

The surly, unshaven bartender came over, plopped a shot glass in front of Ridge, and sloshed it full of whiskey from a greasy, unlabeled bottle. "Four bits," he said.

Ridge eyed the tiny glass skeptically and then looked up at the bartender. "Must be pure bonded sippin' whiskey at them prices," he said.

"It's rotgut, mister, but the price is four bits anyway," the bartender growled. "Take it or leave it."

Ridge pulled out a dollar and dropped it on the bar, then picked up the shot glass and slugged its contents down. The bartender had spoken the truth. It tasted like it had been made the day before and aged all night in a chamber pot. Ridge set the glass down on the bar and motioned for the bartender to pour again.

The bartender splashed the glass full again, spilling more than he got in the glass. Then he picked up Ridge's dollar and started away.

Ridge nursed this drink, sipping on it as he turned his back to the bar and looked out across the room. The air in here was filled with the stench of cheap booze, strong tobacco, and unwashed bodies. Most of the dozen or so conversations going on around him had something to do with gold, mining, gambling, or women. Toward the back of the room eight men were playing cards at a large round table and the only two women in the place, both portly, frowsy floozies, were devoting their attention to the two biggest winners in the game.

A few feet down the bar from Ridge a man clunked his glass on the bar to signal the bartender, then coughed, hawked, spat on the floor, and said, "Claimed it assayed out at nearly a hunnert a ton." He was speaking to the man beside him, who seemed only slightly interested in listening. "Not too bad, really. Worth workin' for shore, but some bastard drilled him 'fore we could get the partnership worked out, an' him the onliest one that knowed where the diggin's was."

"Yeh, that's rotten luck, all right," the other man agreed without enthusiasm. "No idee where it was a'tall, huh?"

"Only that he come in straight from the east," the first man said. "Leastways I got thirty-five dollars out of the deal when I sold his pack an' burro. Seemed like he owed me that much anyway for gettin' his danged self killed 'fore he could make me rich."

"Some folks is jus' plumb inconsiderate that way," the second man said with a sarcasm that was lost on his nearly drunk companion.

Carrying his half-empty glass, Ridge ambled back toward the card game. As he neared, both women appraised him with quick glances, were not impressed with what they saw, and stayed with the men they already had.

Ridge grinned wryly. He had never been the type that women flocked around, especially the saloon women who went for fancy clothes, smooth good looks, and free-flowing cash.

He was a tall man, about six foot one, but he seldom gave the impression of being particularly tall because of the casual slouch of his lean, muscular frame. There was an easy smoothness to his movements; he seldom hurried, but when the time came for action, his decisions and reflexes were lightning quick.

He wore simple cowboy garb — heavy cotton shirt, denim trousers, bandanna, and well-worn boots. He wore the holster of his Colt revolver tied down low, but few people took him for a gunfighter. He looked like a man who was ready for trouble, but not one who went out looking for it.

If there was anything noteworthy about Ridge Parkman's face, it was the good-natured grin that could usually be found there. He liked people and enjoyed making new acquaintances. But the grin could be deceptive, too. It seldom reflected any rapid changes in his temperament. In anger the grin did not fade, but merely got a little crooked and somehow more intense.

When Ridge reached the card table, he stopped behind one player to watch the deal and the first bets. After a moment, however, the man in front of Ridge laid his cards face down, turned to look Ridge in the eye, and barked, "Git!"

Ridge eyed the man's burly shoulders, the dwindling stack of money in front of him, and the nearly empty whiskey bottle nearby. The place where he stood, he decided, wasn't worth fighting to keep. He moved around the table and stood behind a winner who did not seem to mind if half the town watched over his shoulder.

After watching a few hands in the small-stakes game, Ridge realized that the man who had ordered him away was clumsily dealing off the bottom of the deck, but since he was losing anyway, Ridge saw no good reason to make mention of it. In a few minutes he lost interest and started back toward the front of the saloon. He downed the last of the cheap whiskey, left the glass on the bar, and went outside.

Untying President Grant from the hitching rail, he started back down to the main part of town to rejoin the three miners.

He had walked halfway down the street

toward the express office when he saw a crowd gathering about fifty yards ahead of him. Something interesting was happening up there, but he could not yet see beyond the thirty or forty men to find out what it was.

When he reached the edge of the crowd, he looped the horse's reins around a nearby rail and began working his way through the crowd. From the excited laughter and shouted encouragement of the others, he decided a fight must be starting.

As he shouldered his way to the front of the jam of men, he spotted the combatants. His new friend Dolf was backed up against a wagon, and four men, all drunk and growling their anger at the miner, had formed a semicircle around him and were closing in fast. Behind and to one side of Dolf, huddled against a wheel of the wagon, was a young woman about twenty years old.

Dodging a desperate punch from Dolf, one of the attackers grabbed the miner's arm and another quickly leaped forward to get his other arm. Then a third man bravely began working over Dolf's head with a series of brutal punches.

Ridge let the beating continue only for an instant before stepping in to help. He swung one fist in a roundhouse punch and put the man who was beating Dolf out of commission with a crashing blow to the side of his head. As that man fell away in a stupor, the heel of Ridge's boot connected with the midsection of the man who held Dolf's right arm. The snapping of ribs and the huff of air leaving the man's chest sounded simultaneously. He doubled over and dropped weakly to his knees.

With one arm free, Dolf swung wildly and his fist smashed into the face of the man who held his other arm. He staggered back into the arms of the fourth attacker and the two of them quickly backed away and pushed into the crowd, abandoning their downed companions without even a backward glance.

Dolf whirled, furious now and ready to continue the fight, but there was nobody left standing for him to attack.

"Dolf, you got a real talent for gettin' yourself in trouble," Ridge grinned at the angry Dutchman. "Is it somethin' you had to work at or did it jus' come natural?"

"I had to teach them the difference between a real lady an' the barroom chippies they usually meet in these mining camps," Dolf said angrily.

"Wal, they 'bout taught you somethin', too," Ridge said. "But you had the right idea

31

anyway." He turned and for the first time took a close look at the young woman Dolf had been trying to protect. She was splashed with mud and her face was ashen from the shock of what she had just witnessed, but Ridge could still see why Dolf had so readily taken on four men in her behalf.

The waves of her long blond hair outlined a strikingly pretty face with pale cheeks and sparkling blue eyes. She wore a lacy blue dress, which, though it was buttoned modestly up to her throat, still revealed a slim, attractive figure with all the curves in just the right places.

The crowd was already starting to break up as Ridge and Dolf went over to the girl.

"Thank you, both of you," she said. "I don't know what I would have done if you had not come along." Despite a slight quavering, her voice was soft and melodic.

"Dolf did most of the savin'," Ridge said, removing his dusty hat. "But what in tarnation is a snip of a girl like you doin' in a hole like this anyway?"

"I live here with my father," she said defensively. "His name is Herbert Reynolds and he owns the DeWitt's Strike Freight Company. My name is Marjorie Reynolds."

"Miss Reynolds, my name is Adolph Rieger and this is Ridge Parkman. Would you allow us to walk you to wherever you're going?" Dolf asked.

Ridge looked at his new friend with surprise and amusement. Speaking to the girl, Dolf's whole personality changed. He lost the antagonism that seemed to accompany his every word and he addressed her with an almost formal courtesy. His bleeding nose and bruised face detracted from the formal air he adopted, but Marjorie did not seem to notice.

"I would be very grateful if you gentlemen would walk with me to my father's office," she said. "I'm a little shaken by this whole thing. Heaven knows I should be getting used to it after four months here, but I guess I still haven't."

When they reached the freight office, the girl was admitted past a heavy locked door into the back of the building and Ridge and Dolf joined Abe and Oak. The two miners were still carefully selecting the supplies and tools they needed from the piles of goods that had been unloaded on tables inside the large front room of the building.

Abe was just getting interested in badgering Dolf about the condition of his face when Marjorie emerged from the door in back, now accompanied by a middle-aged man in a brown vested suit. When they reached Ridge and the three miners, she said, "These are the men, Dad. I'm afraid I'm responsible for this gentleman's cuts and bruises."

Dolf touched his swelling cheek self-consciously and said nothing.

"Sir, you have my gratitude," Herbert Reynolds told Dolf, extending his hand to the miner. "We're all too short on gentlemen here in DeWitt's Strike, but we have an abundance of cads."

"Must be a rough place for a lady," Dolf agreed. "I'm sorry it happened."

"It would have been much worse if you had not come along," Marjorie insisted. "Please come back in the office and let me tend to your cuts. It's the least I can do."

Dolf argued that they were nothing to bother with, bu he still allowed himself to be led away to the back office by the girl.

"You must have your hands full watchin' out for that daughter of yours," Ridge said to Reynolds. "What with the men round here bein' so starved for the attentions of a woman, I bet trouble comes to her like gnats on a peach."

"It's a serious problem," Reynolds agreed. "Just one of many. But perhaps I won't have to worry about any of it very much longer." His voice trailed off and a serious, worried expression crossed his face.

"How's that?" Ridge asked.

"It's just that so many things are going wrong," Reynolds complained. "This should be a very successful business I have here, with the gold flowing in from these mountains every day and the miners constantly in need of more and more supplies and equipment, but the gold doesn't do anybody any good if we can't get it out to safety. We've appealed to the authorities, but so far they haven't seen fit to send us any help. When the gold isn't stacking up here costing me a fortune for guards, it's being stolen on the trail by outlaws."

"It's a mess all right," Ridge agreed, "but maybe things'll get better 'fore too long."

"Maybe," Reynolds said without conviction. "Maybe they will, and maybe they'll just keep on getting worse."

As the two of them talked, Abe and Oak continued selecting what they needed. By the time Dolf came out of the back room, Abe was dickering with the clerk over how much cash they had coming and Oak was carrying the last of their purchases out to the wagon. Within a few minutes Ridge and the three miners had bid Reynolds and his daughter good-bye and left the freight office.

"Wal, we cashed in at eighty-four dollars," Abe told Dolf. "Me an' Oak spent seventy-six of it whilst you was out fightin' an' courtin'." His baiting drew only an angry glance from Dolf. "That leaves us, as I calc'late, eight bucks for some other necessaries." His glance roamed wistfully down the street toward the Last Nuggett.

"First we eat," Dolf proclaimed. "We couldn't never buy enough whiskey to fill that gut of yours, ol' man, 'less it gets some meat an' beans in it first."

The four of them went down the street to an eatery set up under a huge canvas tarpaulin. The sides of the shelter were rolled up, revealing several long tables and benches lined with men, all stashing away huge amounts of food as quickly as the army of waiters could bring it out from the kitchen.

Instead of going in the front entrance of the tent as Ridge expected, the miners headed around to the back. Behind the tent, garbage and refuse from the kitchen were heaped up in big rotting piles as high as a man's head. Thick columns of wood smoke poured forth out of two flues protruding from the canvas roof, and from inside came the clatter and shouting of the busy crew of cooks and waiters.

When they reached the back entrance to

the tent, Abe stuck his head inside and said, "Hey, they's four hungry men out here needin' some chow."

In a moment a big, burly man parted the back flaps and scowled at the group. He was stripped to the waist and his face, arms, and barrel-shaped chest glistened with sweat. "You three kin go round front an' eat with the white folks," he growled, indicating Abe, Dolf, and Ridge. "I'll put somethin' out here for the Injun boy when I get the chance."

Ridge realized then why they had come to the rear entrance. This place, as was probably the case with all the other restaurants and saloons in town, would not allow Indians to come inside. Out of the corner of his eye Ridge glanced at Oak, but the tall, silent Indian gave no indication that the big man had any effect on him.

"We eat together," Dolf said sourly.

"Shore we do," Abe agreed. "He's our pardner. Jus' bring us some grub out here."

"Suit your own damn selves," the cook said, turning back inside the tent. He soon reappeared carrying a plate with four big hunks of half-cooked steak on it and a steaming pot of red beans. On a second trip he brought them a bucket of coffee, plates, cups, and knives. "Buck an' a half each," he said. "Six dollars all told."

Abe paid and the four of them carried their meal around the side of the tent away from the heaps of garbage and blowing smoke. They all sat cross-legged on the ground and started in on the food.

Ridge took a sip from his cup of coffee and said, "Whew! I thought there wasn't no way to make coffee worse than mine, but they done it. You could float horseshoes in this stuff."

"Good," Dolf said. "Maybe if it's strong enough it'll hide the taste of this food."

"Yeh. Wait'll you try the steak, Ridge."

Parkman cut off a piece of the meat and put it in his mouth, then made a face. "This was *beef* steak we bought, ain't it? I mean, there hasn't been no unusual amount of horses or mules disappearin' round town, has there?"

"A feller learns not to ask too many questions in a place like this. Sometimes the answers is hard on the digestion."

Looking over at the Indian, who was eating quickly and steadily, Ridge said, "Leastways, Oak don't seem to be havin' no trouble with this feast."

"He eats anything," Dolf said.

Oak laid his slab of meat back on his plate and looked up at the others. "When I was a boy," he said, "the Indian agent on the reservation used to hire us to kill the rats in his supply room with sticks, and then we would carry the dead rats home for our family to eat." He said no more, but scooped up some beans with his fingers and put them in his mouth, then took a drink of the hot coffee.

"Didn't mean to make no fun, Oak," Ridge apologized. "I reckon I've et a lot worse than this myself plenty of times, an' been glad to get it, too."

"Ol' Oak, here, he's plannin' to spend his share of the earnin's on cattle to take back to the reservation. Says he wants to get 'em some herds started on their own so's they don't have to rely on no charity from them damn crooked gov'ment men."

"For every cow they deliver to my people," Oak said bitterly, "the agents steal two more from what we are supposed to get and sell them in Texas or Mexico. And while they do this, the children and the old ones die of hunger."

"It's an honorable thing you're doin' an' I admire you for it," Ridge said.

"But none of us are going to make any money or do the things we want if somebody doesn't put a stop to these raiders," Dolf said.

"I reckon from what that Reynolds feller said," Ridge said, "these holdups must be a right big problem round here."

"You betcha they are," Abe agreed. "The way you found us up there on the trail, that's gen'rally the way things is mos' of the time. The damn blood-suckin' no-goods is swarmin' round this place like a lot of wolves, doin' jus' 'bout what they want when an' where they want. Men gotta team up jus' to stay alive. One man on his own ain't got a hope in hell of even livin', let alone diggin' no gold outa the mountain."

"It's always that way round these gold camps," Ridge agreed, "but it does seem the worst here I've ever seen it."

"It's bad all right," Dolf said. "Hasn't been a gold shipment made it down to Adobe City in near two months. We ain't lost nothin' yet 'cause we ain't made no strike big enough to ship, but some of the miners that's makin' good are mad as hell about it. Seems like the gov'ment would send us some help up here, but they haven't done one danged thing."

Ridge nodded his sympathy and kept his mouth shut about his purpose in being in DeWitt's Strike. He was not yet ready to tell even these three men who he was or why he had come here. They would probably only laugh if he explained that he was a deputy U.S. marshal and that his superiors had sent him to DeWitt's Strike to put a stop to the robberies and murders here.

But he wasn't really afraid of their scorn. He had other reasons for keeping his identity secret a while longer. In his years of serving as a deputy marshal, he had learned that it was usually better to keep his identity as a lawman hidden for as long as possible. Not only did a badge on his chest make him a tempting target for every gunslinger and reputation-hungry killer in the area, but it also seemed to have the effect of shutting up a lot of people who might otherwise give him valuable information. As long as he appeared to be just an ordinary drifter, tongues were looser and he was able to move around with much more freedom.

"It's a fact that the gov'ment don't seem to give a hoot whether we sink or swim up here," Abe said. "There's been several calls went out for troops or marshals to come in here an' protect the gold, but they've left us on our own so far."

"Why don't the local people here do somethin' to stop it all themselves?" Ridge asked. "Reynolds won't be able to do it all by himself an' pay for everything out of his own pocket."

"Oh, they's been talk in town 'bout electin' some town marshals, but ain't nobody come along that's a big enough fool to want that job yet."

One's here now, Ridge thought wryly.

"Folks do catch a thief or a claim jumper now'n then, though, an' jumpin' catfish, when they do it's a sight to behold. The last one they caught, by the time the mob got 'im strung up from a rafter in the livery barn, they was so worked up that they jus' went ahead an' burned the livery barn down on top of him. Later everybody passed the hat to pay Jonah Pendleton for his burnt down barn, but that night somebody slit ol' Jonah's throat an' stole that money from him. I mean to tell you, it's a helluva town."

They soon finished their supper and turned the eating utensils in at the back of the tent. Abe was gnashing at the bit to head for the nearest saloon and blow their last two dollars, but before he and Dolf started away, he gave Ridge hurried instructions about how to get to their mine, the Pipe Dream.

"We'd be proud to put you up for a night or two if you get up our way, Ridge, but you watch out for yourself ridin' round in these here mountains. It ain't safe a'tall for a man by hisself."

"I'll keep an eye out," Ridge promised.

After Abe and Dolf had gone, Ridge walked back with Oak to the wagon. The Indian seemed to have no interest in whiskey and Ridge knew it was wise for one of the three miners to guard their supplies now that night was falling and the town was really getting rowdy.

"Don't s'pose there's any decent place for a man to bed down in this town, is there?" Ridge asked the Indian.

"There are the tent houses," Oak told him. "Many beds and many men."

"That's what I thought," Ridge said. "Wal, I don't have no strong urge to sleep on a cot with fifty other stinkin' snorin' men while somebody's outside stealin' my horse an' saddle. Reckon I'll take to the hills."

He walked down the street to where he had left his horse tied an hour or so earlier before the fight. He mounted up and turned President Grant north, heading back out of town in the direction they had entered earlier. Within half an hour he had found himself a campsite with enough nearby grass for the horse and enough cover for Ridge to feel reasonably secure as he bedded down for the night.

CHAPTER 3

Parkman paused on the board sidewalk in front of the Last Nuggett to wait for the carpenter's wagon to rumble past, headed toward the cemetery at the edge of town. As it rolled by he glanced at the two plank coffins in back and shook his head. He had seen those men die the night before, guns blasting with drunken fury as they fought in the middle of the street over the favors of a fallen dove from one of the saloons.

During his first week in DeWitt's Strike, that wagon making its morbid daily journey had become a familiar sight to Ridge. Seldom had there been a morning when the carpenter had not had to box up and bury the casualties of senseless fights, robberies, and attacks of the night before. It was a wild and woolly little town, a place where a man had to keep his wits about him constantly.

Ridge had kept a low profile during his stay in town. Since he never got drunk and went out of his way to avoid trouble, he was still a fairly anonymous figure amid the bustle of activity. He was known in the saloons around town where he spent a lot of time buying drinks to loosen tongues, but most of the bartenders had him tagged as just another shiftless drifter passing time and looking for some way to get his hands on a little cash without working too hard for it. The saloon girls knew him well enough to know that he was seldom good for more than one drink a night and could never be persuaded to make a trip out back with them.

But he had gathered a little bit of important information in town. Perhaps most important was the fact that the thieves never seemed to miss a gold shipment, even those that left in the dead of night. Ridge thought that they might be getting some sort of advance information, perhaps from some of the guards who worked for the freight company, or even, possibly from some of the company management.

He had tried to find out something about the company owner, Herbert Reynolds, and his manager and right-hand man, Max Bramwell, but nobody in town knew much about either of them. Reynolds had come here and started the company a few months before, but nobody seemed to know where he was from. Soon after his arrival, Reynolds had hired Bramwell to help him manage the employees and handle the arrangements for the shipments of gold and freight.

Ridge had not met Bramwell yet, but knew him on sight. He dressed well, bossed his men with a stern hand, and seemed to have set his sights on Marjorie Reynolds, who was perhaps the only respectable woman in town.

When the burial wagon was past, Ridge stepped off the boardwalk and started down the street. He liked the town a little better in the morning and was usually out and about early before the streets and businesses became crowded and the chaos began again. He had just left the small restaurant where he ate breakfast each day, and he was headed now toward the DeWitt's Strike Freight Company office. The night before he had decided that this was the day he would carry his investigation one step further. It was time to end the talking and nosing around and to start taking action.

A scowling clerk sat behind the counter inside the front door of the freight company office. His eyes were red and puffy and his face was drawn in a morning-after-a-hard-night look. He was leaning back in his chair

46

with a Winchester cradled across his lap. As Ridge walked up to the counter, the man's hand went down to rest lightly near the trigger of the weapon.

"I need to see your boss," Ridge said, putting on an easy grin and keeping his hands in plain sight above the counter.

"What about?" the man asked cautiously. Security was tight here because this was the closest thing to a bank in town and Reynolds wanted to discourage anybody who might have the idea of helping himself to the gold that was stored there.

" 'Bout a job," Ridge said. "I hear they might be hirin'."

"They're always hirin' here," the man said with an odd chuckle that contained no trace of humor. "Guess you might say this outfit's got a real steady turnover." He reached up and pulled on a cord which hung down behind him from the ceiling, and Ridge heard the faint ring of a bell in back.

In a moment a small window in the door at the rear of the room opened and a rifle muzzle stuck out a few inches. Then a face appeared and glanced around the room cautiously before the eyes came to rest on Ridge.

"Wants to see the boss," the clerk called back to the man at the door.

"All right," the man said gruffly. "Leave the iron up front, mister, an' come on back."

Ridge unstrapped his gun belt and handed it across to the clerk, then walked back to the door. Though he had never been back there, he had heard of the armed guards in the back of the shipping company and was careful not to make any sudden moves as he went through the doorway.

The windowless ten-by-ten room contained five men sitting around in various places, each armed with a revolver on his hip and holding a new lever-action Winchester .44 carbine. At the rear of the room was another heavy wooden door, and Ridge guessed that opened into the vault room. Another open door to the right led to what was obviously Reynolds's office.

As the guard was closing and bolting the door behind Ridge, Bramwell stepped to the office door and looked Ridge over quickly. "What you need?" he asked.

"I come lookin' for a job," Ridge told him. Reynolds came to the door and recognized Ridge immediately. "Oh, hello Mr. — I don't believe I caught your name the other day," he said.

"It's Ridge Parkman, but Ridge'll do fine, Mr. Reynolds."

"Come in the office, Ridge," Reynolds

said. "It's all right, Max. This is one of the men I told you about who saved Marjorie from those ruffians the other day."

Ridge entered the office, glad to be out from under the watchful eyes of the several guards. They all looked mean as copper-heads and downright anxious to try out those shiny new carbines.

Reynolds gave Ridge a warm reception, showing him to a chair and pouring him three fingers of whiskey in a glass, but Bramwell did not take part in the welcome. He stood back and eyed the newcomer guardedly.

Ridge took a sip of the drink and looked up appreciatively. "I 'bout forgot what good likker tasted like," he said, "after drinkin' so much of that green gut-grabber these places in town sell."

"Yes, we only haul in barrels of the cheapest whiskey we can find because that's all the saloons here want," Reynolds said. "But I always keep a private stock for myself and my friends. Now what was this about you needing a job?"

"I heard you paid pretty good wages for guards," Ridge said, "an' right now I'm near busted an' lookin' for some way to make a little stake for myself."

"Can you handle a gun, Parkman?" Bramwell asked.

"I been accused of knowin' which end of a six-shooter the bullet comes out of," Ridge grinned.

Bramwell looked at him through cold, expressionless eyes and asked evenly, "Have you ever been accused of bein' a smart-mouthed son of a bitch?"

"A couple of times," Ridge said, his voice lowering to the quiet, throaty tone which close friends knew meant trouble. "But gen'rally the fellers that said it wished later they'd been more friendly."

"Gentlemen, gentlemen," Reynolds interrupted quickly. "There's no need for this kind of exchange." He gave Bramwell a sharp glance and Bramwell said no more. "Now, Ridge," Reynolds went on, "I don't want to lie to you or give you any false impressions. The only jobs I have are for armed guards here at the station and on the wagons that take, or should I say, try to take the gold shipments down to Adobe City. We pay well because it's dangerous work — extremely dangerous work."

"I heard that," Ridge said. "But I like the part about paying well."

"Just so you know what you're getting into," Reynolds told him.

"We've lost eleven men in two months,"

Bramwell said. "That don't count the ones that's been wounded. Eleven dead as a hammer."

"We pay a hundred dollars per run to Adobe City and back," Reynolds said. "Twenty-five dollars when you leave and seventy-five dollars when you get back."

"If you get back," Bramwell said.

Ridge took a thoughtful swallow of the drink, staring at the glass for a moment. He was a little puzzled by Bramwell's obvious attempts to discourage him, but he had already weighed the risks he was taking and was determined to hire on with this company. Finally he looked up at Reynolds and said, "Well, sir, I've got a mind to go out in these mountains an' see if I can't find me some of that gold, but like I said, I'm as broke as a hard-luck sodbuster after a long dry spell. If you'll have me, you got yourselves a man."

Reynolds looked up at Bramwell and Bramwell nodded once to signal his reluctant approval.

"All right, Ridge, you're on the payroll as of now," Reynolds said. He opened a drawer of his desk and took out a $20 gold piece, which he passed across the desk to Ridge. "That should help you get by for now. We'll be in touch."

"That's it?" Ridge asked. "Shouldn't I get my guns an' start guardin' or somethin'?"

"We have enough men here," Reynolds said. "When we get ready to send a shipment out, we call our guards in on a moment's notice, give them their instructions, and send them out immediately. That way no one can get word out to any friends who might be waiting along the trail to rob the wagons. Just stay in town and keep yourself available to leave at any time."

"You're the boss," Ridge said, pocketing the money and rising to leave.

But when he reached the door, Bramwell stopped him. "Just one more thing, Parkman. Not all of those eleven men died from outlaw bullets. A couple of them decided that they weren't earning enough an' tried to get rich quick — but it didn't work."

"I savvy your meaning, Bramwell," Ridge said quietly, "but don't worry. I ain't no thief."

As Ridge left the freight office, the satisfaction that he felt at landing the job was tempered by a certain amount of apprehension about what lay ahead. He knew it was not just generosity that led Reynolds and Bramwell to pay so well for men to make the four-day trip to Adobe City and back.

They had to pay that much to get men who were willing to face the dangers of the trail. From all that Ridge could learn, each of the last four runs from DeWitt's Strike had been robbed and some of the guards had died each time.

It would not be easy, but it was something he was going to have to do if he hoped to learn anything more about the outlaws and how they operated.

He passed up the rows of saloons without stopping in any of them and went to the corrals at the south end of town. On his second day in town he started leaving President Grant at the corrals operated by a Mexican named Gomez, and the next day he began paying Gomez an extra fifty cents a day to let him sleep in the small tack shed near the corrals. Even with its hard dirt floor and the constant odors of horses, sweat-soaked leather, and manure, it was far better than the jammed tent hotels where most of the transients and miners paid a dollar a day to get eight hours' rest on a cot under a canvas roof.

Ridge called President Grant over to the edge of the corral and gave him a penny stick of candy he had bought in town, then went to the shed and got some oats which he fed to the horse from a bucket. He had a sincere affection for the big, gray animal and was always careful to provide him with the best care and feeding available. For a lawman, a dependable horse was a necessary tool of his trade, but Ridge Parkman and President Grant had also become just plain good friends.

After caring for the horse, Ridge went into the shed and got his rifles and a small bundle of gun cleaning gear from his saddlebags. Then he began to break his weapons down one by one and give them a thorough cleaning. A clean, properly operating gun sometimes made the difference between life and death in a desperate situation.

As Ridge was reassembling his Colt, Gomez came walking up from the direction of town. He was a middle-aged man, short and stocky, with a round red face and rows of rotting yellow teeth which he displayed almost constantly with his good-natured grin. He had a strong affinity for liquor and a certain plump senorita who worked in one of the saloons in town, and Ridge suspected that those two pastimes consumed most of the profits from his lucrative livery and horse-trading business.

Gomez walked up to where Ridge was working, looked at his disassembled weapon, and asked, "You plan to shoot someone, senor?"

"I might be goin' to, but I shore hope not," Ridge told him. "I hired myself out to the freight company, an' from what I hear tell, these here guns might come in handy on the trip down to Adobe City."

Gomez's expression become serious when he heard that. "This is a wrong thing you have done, Senor Parkman. The bandidos, they kill many of the guards on those journeys."

"The money's good," Ridge said simply, "an' sometimes a man'll do a lot of damn fool things if the price he's gettin' is right."

"This is true, but still it is not good," Gomez insisted. He started away toward the tack shed, shaking his head at the foolishness of his boarder and mumbling something under his breath in Spanish which could have been admonitions or prayers.

CHAPTER 4

The small draw was only about twice as wide as the heavy freight wagon which was pulled far up into it, out of sight of the trail a few hundred yards away. Ridge Parkman sat on his haunches near the rear of the wagon, smoking cigarettes and listening to the low talk of the six other guards and the wagon driver.

"I think this is a dad-blamed fool idee," Sam, the wagon driver, said, shooting a stream of brown tobacco juice at a six-inch lizard which scurried across some rocks a few feet away. "He's gonna get the whole lot of us kilt, that's what he's gonna do." He was a burly old man with skin like aged leather and a wiry, unkempt salt-and-pepper beard.

"Hell, it might work, Sam," one of the other guards reasoned. "It makes sense that if them bandits hit them other wagons an' don't find no gold, they'd jus' figger there

56

wasn't no gold bein' shipped this trip an' go on back to their hole in the ground. We might pass right on through with nary a shot bein' fired."

The speaker was a man named Rafferty, a tall, lean cowboy-type with an easy drawling speech and a calm expression which never completely left his face even when the worst possibilities were mentioned.

"Shore, an' I might get 'lected the king of England sometime next week, too," the old driver grumbled. "Mark my words, boy. 'Fore this trip is finished, we're gonna get our bee-hinds whopped good an' proper. We shore as hell are."

Ridge did not take part in any of the talk. He preferred to sit back and listen, studying the men he would soon be risking his life alongside.

Two men were sitting on top of the crates of gold in the back of the wagon, cradling their rifles like close friends and waiting out the moments like condemned men straining to hear the footsteps of the executioner. Ridge had heard one of them called Simpson, and the other was called only by his first name, Bobby. Simpson was a short, bulky man with a round, homely face and dull eyes which indicated either a stupid man or one who seldom derived much pleasure or excitement out of life. Bobby was the youngest member of the group, a youth of not more than nineteen or twenty whose wide-eyed, panicky expression showed that he was now having second thoughts about this adventure he had chosen to undertake. He, more than any of the other men, seemed most affected by the dire prophecies and graveyard predictions of old Sam.

At the rear of the wagon were the final three members of the group, one sitting on the tailgate and the other two sitting on the rocks across the ravine from Ridge. The man on the tailgate was named Tyler, an obvious veteran of several of these abortive gold runs down out of the mountains. Though he appeared calm and scoffed quietly to himself each time Sam predicted doom, he displayed his quiet nervousness by rolling and smoking a constant chain of cigarettes.

The men on the rocks, Nimblett and Fawcett, were friends, apparent partners in an abortive mining operation, who were out seeking a new grubstake and a new chance to get rich. They talked mostly among themselves, discussing what supplies they would buy. with their accumulated earnings, and seemed to completely ignore the possibility that they might die trying to earn a new chance for themselves in the gold-fields.

The whole procedure of this trip had been a surprise to Ridge. At dawn that morning when Bramwell had started assembling his drivers and guards for this run, Ridge had felt pretty good about the whole thing. No less than twenty men had been called to the freight office to take the wagons down to Adobe City. It seemed like a force large enough to fight off an attack by anything less than a small army of desperadoes.

But then a few miles out of town Bramwell had pulled the wild card out of his hat. He ordered the last wagon driven off the trail and hidden while the rest of the wagons proceeded on down the trail. His plan might make sense, or it might spell complete disaster for the eight men who stayed behind. This lone wagon contained the entire gold shipment, some $35,000 worth of the yellow stuff, and it was the largest amount yet shipped down in one load.

Bramwell spoke reassuringly to the men who stayed behind. He said if they would wait three hours before getting back on the trail, all the fighting would be finished ahead of them and they could dash through without any trouble. But then, he could afford to be confident about the risks. It was not his gold and he was not going along with the men who were about to take the deadly gamble that he was right. Shortly after the wagon was secured out of sight of the trail, Bramwell mounted up and headed back to DeWitt's Strike.

The group here was tense now. They were armed to the teeth and held their weapons at the ready even now before the journey started. And each time the elderly driver started in on another series of his doomsday prophecies, they began to sweat and squirm a little more. The minutes dragged by like days and the sides of the draw seemed to close in like a vise on the small band.

At last old Sam consulted his battered pocket watch and announced, "Time to make a start, boys. Lord help us, if we live to see the sun set today, we'll have earned our plate of beans."

The men rose stiffly to their feet and began to get into formation as Sam maneuvered the protesting horses and got the wagon out of the ravine. Ridge, riding President Grant, and Rafferty, on a small, agile cow pony, took up their assigned positions on point. Nimblett and Fawcett, riding husky, plodding company horses, trailed along behind the wagon, and Simpson, Tyler, and Bobby took their positions behind the improvised barricades in the back of the wagon.

The first couple of hours of the journey were uneventful as the party passed down the middle of the wide valley. No bandits in their right minds would charge a heavily armed band of men out here in the open, because they could be spotted at least a mile or two away and there was little to hide behind in a pitched battle.

The further they got from town, the less the land was pocked and scarred by the efforts of the gold seekers from DeWitt's Strike. Ridge liked this better. He conceded that gold had a rightful and worthwhile place in the world, but he disliked the condition that gold mining left the land in, and he particularly disliked the fact that anywhere gold was found or mined or stored or hauled or spent, men found countless ways to kill each other off in alarming numbers. It seemed as if every time a man turned around in gold country, somebody else was dead or dying or doing his danged fool best to get killed.

As they drew closer to the series of passes on down the trail, the tension of the men increased noticeably and a cloud of dreary premonition seemed to settle over them.

Several of the eight men had made these runs before, so they well knew what sort of hazards they might be running into. Ridge heard the term "Bloody Run" mentioned several times in ominous tones.

As they entered the first pass, all eyes began roaming up and down the ragged walls of the mountains on each side, straining to spot anything which might give a moment's warning before that first deadly hail of bullets began. Nobody talked now and the eerie silence in the pass was punctuated only by the creek of the wagon and the clatter of the horses' hooves on the rocky trail.

When they had cleared the first pass, the trail widened out again into a small meadow about a hundred yards wide and half a mile long. Then came another pass and another meadow, and so on for several miles as the trail slowly dropped down from the high country. As the hours passed, Ridge began to feel a little better about the trip. For the first time he began to believe that Bramwell's plan might have a chance of working. But none of the other guards had yet voiced any optimism. They still had Bloody Run to go, and nobody was placing any bets until that one great obstacle was behind them.

From what Ridge could tell, if an attack

had not taken place in any of the other passes, Bloody Run, the last and most treacherous pass on the trail, was the most likely spot for the outlaws to make their play.

They started across a small meadow which funneled down ahead into yet another pass. Hunching over as if his shoulders were suddenly laden with an unseen weight, Sam spit his wad of well-chewed tobacco to the ground and growled, "Say your prayers an' cock your hammers, boys. We've reached that damn Bloody Run."

Ridge and Rafferty pulled out ahead a short distance and began craning their necks upward, checking every small crack and crevice in the massive walls of rock on both sides of the trail.

The run was nothing more than a ragged trough through the solid masses of rock. It varied from twenty or thirty yards wide in some places to little more than a wagon's width in others. It was nearly a quarter mile long, all told, but was so crooked that there was scarcely more than fifty yards' visibility ahead in any one place. The walls rose almost straight up one hundred or more feet on both sides.

Ridge and Rafferty checked about the first two hundred yards of the pass, then turned and rode back within sight of the wagon, then turned again and began rechecking the walls of the pass. Ridge cast one quick glance at his companion and saw that Rafferty's teeth were clenched so tightly that his fate was twisted into a snarl. He held his cocked rifle like a pistol, the barrel pointed straight up and ready to be tilted down and fired at anything that moved.

From somewhere out ahead came a sudden ominous howl, a yell distorted by the shape and echo of the pass to the point that it scarcely sounded as if it could have been made by anything human.

Ridge heard Rafferty mutter low and urgently, "Oh, shit! Here it comes!"

In the narrow pass, the exploding dynamite was ear-shattering. The center of the explosion was high up on the rock wall somewhere between the two point men and the wagon, but it was so powerful that hunks of the blasted rock flew with lightning speed toward Ridge and his companion.

There was little time for anything except the split-second realization that this was it. President Grant squealed out, whirled in panic, and went down, hurling Ridge out of the saddle and against the solid wall of stone ten feet away.

It was deathly quiet. Ridge drifted once

toward consciousness, faded back into nothingness, and then finally fought his way to full alertness. His head was pounding brutally and when he tried to open his eyes to look around, he found that one was sealed shut with caked and dried blood. He rubbed the eye with his fingers until he was able to open it, then raised up onto one elbow and looked around.

Tons of rock had tumbled down into the pass near Ridge. The wagon stood where it had stopped a few dozen yards back down the trail. Bracing himself against the stone wall, Ridge struggled to his feet, then stifled a moan as the wound on the side of his head pounded out a fresh wave of pain. A few feet away two startled buzzards abandoned their meal and rose on flapping wings toward the sky. The birds had been battling over the flesh of an arm which protruded from under a pile of stone and rubble. That was Rafferty.

As he staggered back toward the wagon, Ridge spotted the body of Sam slumped awkwardly across the vehicle's horseless singletree. Bobby and Tyler lay dead in the empty wagon bed.

But there were survivors. At the rear of the wagon Ridge found Simpson and Fawcett dozing under an improvised canvas lean-to. Fawcett roused as Ridge neared, but Simpson, badly wounded in the shoulder, did not open his eyes.

"Parkman! You're alive!" the startled Fawcett exclaimed.

"Jus' barely."

"We checked you up there, but it looked to us like your head was busted wide open so we jus' left you layin' there. Sorry."

"It's only half busted, I reckon."

"Nimblett's gone back down the trail to round up some horses," Fawcett said. "Our horses threw us an' run off down that way, so we think the outlaws might not of got 'em. They took the rest."

For the first time Ridge thought of President Grant. He had not seen the big animal dead anywhere so he assumed that the raiders must have taken him, too. At least that meant he was still alive.

"Simpson here's been shot in the shoulder an' I think he's got a busted leg, too. Don't look good for him. I'm all right 'cept for a lot of bruises, an' Nimblett's 'bout the same. Guess you fellers up front caught the worst of it."

"How many of them were there?" Ridge asked.

"A bunch. Maybe twenty-five or thirty," Fawcett said. "After they blasted the damn mountain down on us, they come ridin' in here from the head of the pass an' got the drop on Nimblett an' me 'fore we could say git! These fellers here at the wagon tried to fight it out, but it never was no match. They grabbed the gold an' horses an' rode off in nothin' flat. A real neat job, I gotta say. Didn't none of 'em take a single hit."

Ridge searched the back of the wagon until he found a canteen, then sat down under the canvas with Fawcett. After taking a long drink, he took off his bandanna and began cleaning the crusted blood from his face and hair. With Fawcett's help, he got an adequate bandage made for his head wound.

It was late afternoon when they first began to hear the clatter of hooves up the pass. Soon Nimblett came into sight, riding one horse and leading a second. It was cheering to see him finally return.

"You're a downright welcome sight," Fawcett told the rider, as he brought the horses up to the wagon.

"They didn't like this Bloody Run no better'n we did," Nimblett explained, stepping to the ground. "They run all the way back to that last little meadow an' they was so skittish I had the devil of a time gettin' my hands on 'em."

"So what now?" Ridge asked. "Do we go on to Adobe City or head back to DeWitt's Strike?"

"Seems like we might as well head on down," Nimblett said. "Once we get through a little more rough country on down the way, it's purty easy goin' on into Adobe City. They got a doc there too. Simpson's gonna need one if we can get him there in time."

With that decided, they began the difficult job of clearing the trail enough to get the wagon through. It was backbreaking work for the three battered survivors, but by dark they had enough of the large rocks out of the way to inch the wagon past the rubble. Then they hitched the two horses to the wagon, loaded the dead and wounded in back, and started out.

CHAPTER 5

Adobe City was a welcome sight to the three ragged men who straggled into the city the following afternoon in the empty gold wagon. Simpson, wounded and unconscious in the back of the wagon, had died half a day earlier. The three other men had watched helplessly as his ravings, at first violent, slowly grew weaker and finally ceased altogether, and by the time they reached their destination there were five dead men in the back of the wagon to bury instead of four.

In terms of western settlements, Adobe City was a major metropolis. Its promoters boasted a population of more than five thousand residents and four hundred businesses "supplying every need known to civilized mankind." Fliers sent back east by the bushel to lure prospective migrants to the area promised "plenty of growth and opportunities for all honest, hardworking

69

men and women of true frontier ilk."

Though the city was over fifteen years old, the arrival of the railroad only four years earlier had been the fuse to touch off the boomtown growth in Adobe City. It had become the hub of an ever-widening mining district in the west central part of Colorado, warehousing the goods and equipment shipped in from the east for distribution to the many far-flung towns and mining camps, and gathering up the gold and other mineral treasures in return.

Ridge and his two companions came into town from the north, passing first through the ghetto Mexican quarter on the fringes of the city before reaching the bustling warehouse district which stretched up and down the railroad tracks through the center of town. Fawcett drove the wagon directly to the warehouse where Reynolds's company wagons picked up their loads of goods to carry back to DeWitt's Strike.

When Fawcett, Nimblett, and Parkman reached the warehouse, the men who had gone ahead were all busy loading freight, but they stopped working when the wagon drove up. Joe McKinney, trail boss of the crew, turned back the tarp and took a look at the bloody bodies of the five dead men,

70

muttering a quiet stream of oaths under his breath.

No one asked the survivors for details. The specifics of where and how the robbery had occurred did not matter; what counted was that the gold was gone and five more men were headed to the cemetery in pine boxes.

As one of the other men climbed up on the seat of the wagon to take the reins from Fawcett, Ridge stepped down from the back of the wagon. His head still throbbed from the blow he had received in Bloody Run, but the bleeding had long since stopped and he had decided that the wound was not serious.

The new driver started away, headed for the local undertaker's. Ridge stood around for a few minutes talking to the other men, but the first chance he got, he worked his way to the edge of the group of men and nobody seemed to notice his departure as he rounded a corner of the warehouse and started toward the main part of town.

As he walked down the crowded streets of Adobe City his thoughts were still laden with all that had happened in the last couple of days. Old Sam, Rafferty, Tyler, Bobby, Simpson . . . all were good men. Though Ridge had known them only briefly, he had liked every one. A quick comradeship had formed because of the dangerous job they had undertaken, and Ridge now felt a bitterness eating at him because of their deaths.

When he first rode into DeWitt's Strike, he had merely looked on the assignment as another job he was sent out to do, another tough situation he had to clear up. That was all changed now. Friends had died, and that made this a blood feud. He had a personal stake now in making sure that the members of the outlaw band were killed or brought to justice before they could cause the deaths of any more good men.

And as a final insult, like the last match to set Ridge's anger aflame, he remembered his stolen horse. President Grant was by far the best horse he had ever owned and he was damned if he was going to let some frontier rabble get away with stealing him. When accounting time came, somebody was going to pay a price for that deed, too.

At last he reached the building he was seeking, the big, two-story federal building near the center of town. The fairly new stone structure housed a variety of U.S. government offices including a federal district court, land offices, and a U.S. marshal's office. Cells built into the basement of the building housed the steady stream of prisoners that the deputy marshals were constantly hauling into Adobe City to face justice.

Ridge circled around and entered the building from the rear, not wanting any of his companions to see him go in the front door and later start asking questions. He took the back stairs to the second floor and walked down the hall to the marshal's office.

The front office was empty, but when he closed the door behind him he heard a chair slide back in the inner office and in a moment a man came to the doorway. "Can I help you?" the man asked, not immediately recognizing Ridge through the layers of grime and trail dust.

"I hear there's a tough ol' bird name of Henry Lott doin' some marshalin' in these parts."

"Ridge!" Lott exclaimed, rushing forward to shake Parkman's hand. "I didn't recognize you, son. You look like you got aholt of the fightin' end of a mountain grizzly an' couldn't let go."

"I wish that's all it was, Henry. I come down from DeWitt's Strike ridin' shotgun on a gold shipment an' we got ourselves ambushed. Lost five men an' a whole wagonful of the yellow stuff."

As Lott ushered Ridge into the inner office and sat him down in a big leather chair, he said, "I got a wire from Denver that said you'd been put on that DeWitt's Strike case, but I didn't know when you'd get there or when you'd check in with me."

Lott went around and sat down behind his desk, taking a bottle and two glasses out of a cabinet behind him and pouring healthy slugs of whiskey for them. He was a man in his mid-fifties, ruggedly handsome in a cold, stern sort of way. His hard, husky body topped six feet by a comfortable margin, and the only sign of approaching old age was the steely gray in his handlebar mustache and thick dark hair. He sat erect in his chair, his eyes intense and unreadable.

Parkman and Lott's friendship went back through several years and quite a few adventures. They had been together on a couple of operations during the war, and later had ridden partners on a few assignments out west. Though Lott had been forced into accepting a promotion to a desk job a couple of years before, he still much preferred the field work, and Ridge readily admitted that he was one of the sharpest and most competent men he had ever worked alongside.

Ridge accepted his drink and slid down tiredly in the seat as he took the first swallow, letting the smooth golden liquor scour out the dry taste of trail dust from his mouth. "It was a plumb miserable situation, Henry," Ridge said finally. "We got whipped like puppies in a wolf pack. It was in a place called Bloody Run, an' they blasted the sides of it down on us to sort of soften us up 'fore they come ridin' in an' took the gold."

Lott sat back in his chair, nodding occasionally but seldom speaking as Ridge went through the details of the robbery. At last Ridge finished with an account of the long ride into Adobe City and the death of Simpson.

As Lott poured Parkman a second drink and refilled his own glass, he said, "So we almost lost us a deputy marshal out there, huh?"

"You sure as hell come close."

"Well, did you learn anything that might help us track them down?"

"Not one helluva lot," Ridge conceded. "But there was one thing about the attack that might deserve some checkin'." He told Lott about the unsuccessful plan to send the decoy wagons on ahead of the real shipment and about how the first wagons had gotten through without harm. "They knew ahead what the plan was an' which of us to hit," Ridge said with conviction.

"So somebody who is in on the planning of the gold shipments is sending word out to the outlaws?" Lott asked.

"I'm convinced of it. There's three men I know of who might have known the plan far enough ahead to have sent word out to the raiders. One is the company owner, a man named Herbert Reynolds, and another is his manager, a slicker named Max Bramwell. The last one is Joe McKinney. He's the trail boss. There could be some others in the company that I don't know about, but them three for sure musta known how it was gonna be done."

Lott wrote the names of the three men down on a piece of paper and then asked Ridge for a complete physical description of each man. "Well," he said finally, "these names will give me somethin' to start on. I can send them out on the wire an' see if Denver or Washington's got any files on them. Anything else?"

"No, 'cept that I sure could use some help on this one," Ridge said.

"Yeh, I know, Ridge," Lott said, "but it's the same ol' story. You've heard it a hundred times before. Not enough men . . . not enough money . . . an' too many hundreds of square miles full of backshooters, renegades, rapists, whiskey peddlers, con men, gunfighters . . . you name it. That's why I had to get somebody sent over from Denver to look into this DeWitt's Strike mess in the first place. Right now I don't have a single man I could send up there, but some-thin' has to be done fast.

"I can promise you this, though, Ridge. I've worked out a deal with Captain Halli-burton to get troops when an' if we find out who these raiders are an' where they're hidin' out at. We can draw from the garrison right here in Adobe City, but only for short, specific operations."

"Fine, Henry," Ridge said. "It looks like it'll take an army to round up this bunch. There's a passel of 'em for shore. As far as the check on those names I gave you, I don't know when I'll get back down here, but maybe I can find somebody to send down here after it."

"I should have some answers for you in about a week."

"Good."

They talked for a few more minutes, but Ridge knew he should not stay away from the wagons too long. McKinney or some of the others might miss him and start asking questions when he got back.

Finally, swallowing the last of the whiskey,

Ridge shook Lott's hand and left, going down the back stairs and out the back door. In a few minutes he was back at the wagons and nobody seemed to notice his absence.

Though the wagons were only about half loaded, the other guards and drivers were sitting around doing nothing. Ridge joined a group of four men who were sitting on the ground on the shady side of one wagon. As he took out the makings and began building himself a smoke, the other men continued their conversation.

"I knew this had to happen one time or 'nother," one man said. "Next thing you know, they'll start tryin' to welch on our wages."

"Wal, you can't blame 'em," a companion reasoned. "Can't expect these wholesalers to keep on supplyin' ol' man Reynolds an' the whole town on credit when there ain't one single nugget gettin' down from the hills to pay 'em with."

"It's a bitch, ain't it? All that gold up there an' these goods down here, an' none of it ain't doin' nobody no good with them back-shootin' belly crawlers in between."

"Yeh, it stinks."

As they talked, Joe McKinney walked over to them from the warehouse office, a mighty scowl on his face. The men looked up and one of them asked, "How about it, Joe? They gonna let us fill out the load?"

"Hell no," McKinney growled. "They say they're paperin' their walls with DeWitt's Strike Freight IOUs an' they won't give us no more than jus' foodstuffs to take back with us 'til they start seein' gold come down off that mountain."

"Ol' man Reynolds will bust a vein when he hears that."

"Yeh, an' Bramwell ain't exactly goin' to love the news himself," McKinney said.

"So what do we do, Joe?"

"Ain't nothin' we can do but jus' take what they'll give us an' head on back. Ain't our fault that the government won't come in an' clean out that nest of rattlers so we can get a gold shipment through once in a while."

The men returned to the docks and loaded the last of the goods which were to be taken. When that was done, most began to scatter out into town to see how much trouble they could get into before their dawn departure.

Ridge Parkman, however, had a couple of calmer pleasures in mind. Just then the attraction of the Adobe City saloons and bordellos couldn't compete with the anticipated joy of a hot bath and a soft bed.

CHAPTER 6

Max Bramwell stood on the back dock of the freight company building, scowling silently as he watched the men unload the goods from the wagon. He had given them all a pretty hard time earlier in the day when they returned and reported that the gold had not made it through, but by now his tantrum had run its course and he had lapsed into mere sullenness.

It seemed to Ridge Parkman that there was something strange about Bramwell's reaction. Surely the news was not completely unexpected; this kind of thing *had* happened before. Perhaps, Parkman thought, Bramwell acted that way because it had been his idea to send the wagons out the way they did, and now he was acting tough on the guards to cover his own frustration at being wrong.

But there was another possibility. It might all be a fake. If Bramwell was in some way connected with the robberies, the most logical way for him to behave now would be to seem infuriated that another robbery had taken place.

Ridge pitched in with the others to unload the shipment of goods, but he had already decided that he would not be making any more gold runs. A dead deputy marshal could not catch any outlaws, and working for this company was the best way Ridge had discovered locally for a man to get dead real fast.

When all the supplies had been carried into the building, Ridge lined up with the other men to get his pay. Reynolds had agreed to give Ridge a rifle and another horse to replace his stolen mount, and Ridge planned to use his pay to buy himself a prospecting outfit. With that, he could wander the surrounding mountains, coming and going from town as he pleased, without arousing the slightest suspicion about his motives.

When Ridge's turn came at the pay table, Bramwell weighed out $80 in gold and dumped it into a small leather pouch. Gold dust was a common unit of exchange in these mining towns where government coins and scrip were always scarce, and the small scales which measured the weight and value of gold were used in all sorts of businesses from saloons to butcher shops.

"Well, Parkman," Bramwell said. "You got a good taste of what it's like out there. Reckon you're just livin' right or somethin' to make it back alive."

"I was lucky," Ridge said. "But I never did like to stretch my luck no further than I have to. Workin' for this outfit puts me in mind of when a man gets took by the Indians. It ain't really a question of *if* he's gonna die, but just a matter of when an' how. I never did pine to get to be no old man, but I did figger to live jus' awhile longer an' I think workin' here is the wrong way to go about it."

"Some stay on an' some don't," Bramwell said disinterestedly. He turned his attention back to weighing out a measure of gold for the next man in line, and Ridge turned away. He walked over to where his new horse stood and untied the reins from the hitching rail.

It was an adequate horse, a grayish-brown dun, thirteen hands high with a deep chest and strong legs. He was by no means a match for the missing President Grant, but he was far better than any horse Ridge could have hoped to buy in this town for $80 worth of gold. The hostler had told

Ridge the animal's name was Bill.

It was still only midmorning so the streets and saloons had yet to be jammed with the crowds of men who, by late afternoon, would begin another long evening of drinking and hell raising. Ridge stopped in at the Last Nuggett and walked over to the bar for a cup of coffee. He planned to have his outfit bought and be out on the trail before nightfall, but there was time enough for a little relaxation before he got started.

Only half a dozen sullen and bleary-eyed men leaned against the bar inside, and about that many more sat slumped around at the various tables in the room, drinking coffee or liquor and talking very little. None of the dowdy barroom belles had yet appeared this morning.

At the back of the bar a stooped and shuffling man was starting to clean up, scattering buckets of sand on the floor to soak up the accumulated mess of spilled drinks, tobacco spit, and blood before he began sweeping.

As Ridge watched the swamper work, he went over his plans for the next few days. He often preferred to work alone on a case, but occasionally, such as now, that had its drawbacks, too. He had decided to leave town and search for the outlaw hideout, but he also wished he could stay here in town to watch Reynolds, Bramwell, and some of the other men associated with the freight company. He also had another trip to make down to Adobe City sometime soon and that would be another three days that he would be away from DeWitt's Strike.

He knew he definitely needed a man to leave here in town, somebody who knew the town and the people in it, and somebody he was reasonably sure he could trust. That kind of person would not be so easy to find, though. So far the only friends he had made were the three miners, Abe, Dolf, and Oak, and their claim was too far from town for them to be of any use to him.

But, he decided, he would just have to do the best he could with the time he had, and wait for his break to come. He was a patient man, and his patience usually paid off.

The swamper was crossing and recrossing the room, walking backward and scattering the sand from his bucket. When he neared the bar his foot hit one of the grubby spittoons behind him. It turned over and splashed brown ooze onto the boot of one of the sulking drinkers.

The man turned, his face quickly reddening with rage at the swamper's clumsiness. "You worthless ol' gutter rat!" he stormed.

"Why don't you watch what the hell you're doin'?"

The swamper turned and began mumbling his apologies as he bent to set the spittoon upright, but his antagonist was not going to let it go at that. He cuffed the swamper on the side of his head, knocking him to his knees, and said, "Clean that damn boot off."

By then the bartender had noticed the commotion, and he too began to rail at the cleanup man. "Dammit, Mike, can't you do nothin' right? Here I give you a chance to make a little change an' you up an' start splashin' the spit buckets all over my customers."

Mike did not bother to look up or answer as he took a corner of his filthy shirttail and began dabbing at the offended boot. When he was finished, the man lifted his foot and gave Mike a shove, sprawling him back on the floor. He was stepping forward to land a kick when Ridge decided that this fellow was beginning to get in a few more licks than he deserved.

"Ain't a whole lot of use doin' no more to him," Ridge reasoned to the angry man. "It ain't like he done somethin' so terrible."

The kick never fell as the man turned angrily to Ridge and said, "Nobody asked you to stick your nose into this business, mister. It ain't none of your concern."

"I'm makin' it my concern," Ridge said quietly, an edge of warning creeping into his voice. "Let him be."

Without warning the man swung a fist in Ridge's direction, but Ridge had been expecting that to happen any time and easily shoved the swing aside with his left forearm. He jabbed out a quick hard punch with his own right fist. The blow landed squarely on the man's mouth, knocking him back across the spittoon and sprawling him onto his back on the floor. Clumsily he reached for the holstered revolver on his hip.

"Don't!" Ridge snapped. "Ain't no use you dyin' over a little thing like this."

The man hesitated, and then his hand left the vicinity of his gun as he realized that drawing now would almost certainly cause his death.

"You get the hell outa my place," the bartender growled at Ridge. "An' you get out too, Mike. I don't need no clumsy ol' drunk like you doin' more harm than you do good."

Ridge glanced quickly at the bartender and the man he had knocked down, then his eyes went to Mike, who was still sitting on the floor. "You go out first, Mike," he said, "while I linger here an' make sure our friend keeps his seat 'til we get clear of this place."

The swamper got up and started toward the door, then Ridge backed out, his gaze remaining steadily on his downed opponent.

When he got outside, Ridge relaxed some. Little situations like that too often flared up into full-fledged shoot-outs, and he counted himself lucky that he did not have to leave a dead man in there on the floor instead of just a bully with his pride wounded.

When he looked around, Mike had already rounded the corner of the building and started away. Ridge hurried to catch up with him.

"Hey," he said, catching the man's arm and stopping him. "You all right, mister?"

"Frank owed me two days' wages," Mike grumbled sullenly. "Dollar fifty . . . an' you lost it for me."

"Wal, don't get carried away with gratitude jus' 'cause I saved you from a beatin'," Ridge snapped.

"He give me whiskey sometimes, too," Mike mourned. "Eight, ten drinks some nights, an' I got to eat from the free lunch table."

"Wal, I'll be damned," Ridge muttered to himself. "Serves me right, I guess, for buttin' in. Sorry."

"Jus' gimme a dollar an' we'll call it even," Mike told him.

"I will be damned," Ridge repeated. He stared at Mike a moment and then came to a decision. "Come on. I won't give you no drinkin' money, but I will buy you a meal if you ain't let that rotgut eat too many holes in your belly to hold food."

Mike seemed about to protest, but Ridge held him by the upper arm and steered him toward the street. As they rounded the corner of the saloon, Ridge glanced around cautiously to make sure the man he knocked down was not waiting there for him, but the boardwalk and the street beyond were deserted.

Ridge led Mike down the street and into the first eating place they came to. Soon after they were seated, a waiter came over to them. He looked at Mike with obvious disgust, then turned to Ridge and said, "He ain't never got no money, mister."

"I'm buyin' for the both of us," Ridge said. "Jus' bring us some steak an' beans an' coffee. Plenty of coffee. Okay?"

The waiter shrugged his shoulders and started away toward the kitchen. When he was gone, Ridge turned and surveyed his companion. It was not uncommon for most men to carry a smell around with them from days or weeks of working and never taking a bath, but the variety and intensity of the smells that came from this Mike character were incredible. His ragged, threadbare clothes were so filthy that it was impossible to tell what color they had originally been, and his body was so layered with accumulated dirt that he had actually started to peel in places. Under his shapeless hat his hair was a tangled, greasy mat.

But what was equally depressing to Ridge as the man's slovenly and disgraceful appearance, was his spiritless, handdog attitude. He seemed to accept cruelty or kindness, pleasure or pain, with the same passive resignation. Ridge guessed that the only thing that would probably stir any signs of enthusiasm in this man might be the mention or promise of a drink of whiskey.

"My name's Ridge Parkman," Ridge said finally. When the other man made no response except a vague nod, he asked, "An' you're Mike what?"

"Mike DeWitt."

"DeWitt? Same as the town here? Same as DeWitt's Strike?"

"Yeh. I was the first one here."

"You mean this place is named after you?" Ridge asked in amazement.

"Yeh. I was the first one found colors here. In that stream over there no more'n a hunnert yards from where we're sittin' right now." For the first time he was beginning to show a spark of life and emotion. "I opened up the first mine in these parts, too, right up there on that mountain. But it's all gone now. Vein played out."

Ridge leaned back in his chair, partly to study his companion and partly to put his nose a few more inches away from the waves of stench that filled the air around DeWitt

He found this revelation incredible. Most of these little mining towns were either named after a local landmark or one of the first prospectors in the area, but it was amazing to think that this settlement was named after a man who was now one of its most miserable residents. Ridge felt a wave of pity for DeWitt. It would be bad enough to turn into a worthless drunk anywhere, but to discover such a gold-laden area as this one and then to become a drunk while others got rich seemed an unbelievably cruel irony.

Ridge got DeWitt to choke down about half of his meal through a combination of cajolery and threats. All through the meal Ridge kept thinking that here could be the man he needed if only he was not a drunkard. Who would know more about what was going on in a town than its first resident?

But as a drunken, smelly bum, Mike was not going to be any use to anybody. Ridge decided that he would first try to get Mike cleaned up and sobered up, and then try to find out if he had sense enough about him to be of any use in the search for the raiders.

The food had an almost immediate effect on DeWitt. As they sat at the table drinking cup after cup of coffee, he began to talk more and the things he said started making more sense. Soon Ridge had him talking about how he had come to be here and how he had eventually ended up in the shape he was now in.

Working his way north out of Adobe City several months earlier, DeWitt had hit upon what appeared to be a fairly rich vein of gold on the mountainside almost directly above where the town now stood. He had worked the claim secretly for a while, but at last when he took a healthy amount of gold down to Adobe City to cash it in, word got out. A few fortune hunters trailed him back to this area, and within a few weeks a gold rush was on. The town sprang up overnight and the hills were soon crawling with prospectors.

But while the town which bore his name was just beginning to thrive and other men were starting to get rich in the gold mining district which he discovered, fate was preparing to overwhelm Mike DeWitt.

He had been a hard-luck drifter all his life, always roaming and seldom possessing more than one horse or mule and a few dollars, so when his mine started paying off, he started living the good life. He spent every cent as soon as he got his hands on it, confident that the vein would go on and on and that he would get richer and richer.

Then one day he blasted a few feet further back into the mountain and the vein ended suddenly, sheared off by an ancient upheaval millions of years before.

DeWitt kept on working the claim for a while, desperately running shafts this way and that in futile attempts to relocate the vein. But as his debts mounted and his discouragement grew, he began to spend more and more time each day in the saloons in town and less time working the mine. At last the whiskey took over and he became a hopeless drunk, a broken-spirited man whose dreams of wealth and comfort had been snatched away from him.

That was the man Ridge had saved from a kick in a barroom, the man who swabbed up spit with his own shirttail.

At last Ridge paid the tab and they left the restaurant. As they started down the street, Ridge told his companion, "I'm gonna pay for a bath an' a new change of clothes for you, Mike. You stink like last year's outhouse. I don't see how a man could let himself get so filthy an' still bear to live inside his own skin."

"I don't need your bath none nor your clothes," DeWitt grumbled. "Jus' leave me alone an' maybe I can get on in one of the other saloons."

Ridge turned to DeWitt, and though he was grinning, there was no mistaking the determination in his voice. "I don't 'member askin' you if you wanted a bath. I jus' said you was gettin' one."

DeWitt thought about that for a moment, then said, "Look, Parkman, I 'preciate your intentions, but it won't do no good. I done tried it before. The bath, a shave, clean clothes an' all, but I always ended up stinkin' drunk an' passed out back of some saloon 'fore the night was over. Jus' lemme be. Every town's gotta have a town drunk."

But still DeWitt went along with Ridge, and he stood docilely nearby while Ridge dickered with the two Mexicans who ran the bathhouse they came to.

"My friend here don't seem to be very fond of soap an' water," Ridge told the two men, "so maybe you might have to give him sort of a hand."

The two surveyed DeWitt with gleaming eyes and smiling faces, anxious to earn the extra fifty cents apiece that Ridge promised them if DeWitt was clean when he got back.

An hour later, scrubbed, shaved, and dressed in the outfit of secondhand clothes which Ridge bought for him, Mike DeWitt was a new man. In appearance, at least, he had returned to the human race.

That day and the next were pretty rough for the miner. Ridge never left his side and they spent most of their time either playing endless hands of cards in Gomez's shed or taking walks around town. On the second morning the shakes and sweats began, but Ridge helped him through the ordeal with patience and firm determination.

By the evening of the second day DeWitt at last began to believe he would live through the experience. For the first time since he had become Parkman's virtual prisoner, he tried eating some of the food which was given to him and, remarkably, was able to keep it in his stomach.

That evening they sat in the shed talking. DeWitt's face was pale and his features were drawn and exhausted looking, but his eyes had lost that lifeless, hopeless dullness which Ridge had seen in them on the first day they met.

DeWitt took another swig of the cup of coffee that Ridge kept constantly filled and in front of him, and his face screwed up into a grimace. "I wouldn't never of guessed that a man could down as much coffee as I have in two days an' not jus' pop his gut," the miner grumbled. "I bet I've put away every bit of five gallons."

"Wal, I've matched you durn near cup for cup," Ridge said.

The past two days had been an ordeal for him, too, but he was proud of what he had accomplished. He thought DeWitt was just about ready.

"You know, Mike," Parkman said, "I've done jus' about all I can. Now it's come time for you to take over. You think you can handle it?"

"I'm gonna take a whack at it, Ridge, but I don't know. I ain't shore. An' I still ain't figgered out why you went an' done all this in the first place."

"I need your help, Mike," Ridge told him. "I need a friend here I can count on."

DeWitt looked at him curiously. "Been a long time since anybody was fool 'nough to

95

try an' count on me."

"You wanta work for me, Mike?"

"Work?" DeWitt asked. "Why? You got some spittoons that need scrubbin'?"

"Catchin' outlaws is the line I'm in," Ridge said bluntly.

DeWitt stared back at him, wondering whether this might be some kind of joke or if perhaps his new friend had suddenly gone mad. "What in the hell you talkin' about?" he asked guardedly.

"I'm a deputy United States marshal," Ridge said. "I've been sent to this town to see if I can't do somethin' about these holdups an' killin's round here, an' I need a helper. I need a good man that I can count on to do what I say when I say. You want that job, Mike?"

DeWitt just stared back at him for a moment. Then he said, "Yeh, I want it, Ridge, but I can't promise you ain't makin' one helluva mistake here."

"I think I'll take my chances with that."

"Okay, Ridge, okay. You got yourself a deppity's deppity. I ain't much of a hand with a gun, but I got myself a rusty ol' Hawken rifle up to the mine. You'll have to buy me some powder an' lead for it, though."

"Naw, Mike," Ridge reassured him.

"There ain't gonna be no shootin' for a while, least I hope not. I'm gonna need your eyes an' ears right here in town, an' I want you to make some trips for me, down to Adobe City an' maybe someplace else." He explained about the information Henry Lott was supposed to be getting for him and told DeWitt that his first job would be to go down and bring it back.

"I reckon I can handle that a'right," De-Witt said. "Don't s'pose none of them owl-hoots would bother wastin' a bullet on my hide."

"That's what I'm countin' on," Ridge admitted. " 'Til I can get a little better idea of what's goin' on round this place an' who's helpin' who steal the gold, I want to keep it a secret who I am an' why I'm here. It makes my job easier."

"You shore had me fooled," DeWitt admitted. "I wouldn't of pegged you for a law-man in a million years."

"Wal I am," Ridge assured him, "an' now, so are you. How does it feel?"

"Not good a'tall," DeWitt admitted. "It's kinda like leanin' out over a cliff an' hopin' nobody behind you gets funny ideas."

"You get used to it after a while," Ridge grinned. "Least that's what they tell me."

CHAPTER 7

Starting at dawn, Ridge rode north out of town, at first following the established trail up the center of the long valley. On the back of his horse was strapped enough prospecting gear to establish him as just another gold seeker in case anybody became curious about why he was roaming the mountains in the vicinity of DeWitt's Strike.

Before leaving town that morning, he had started Mike DeWitt out in the other direction on a rented mule, headed toward Adobe City. DeWitt carried a letter which Ridge had written to Henry Lott, and his instructions were to stay in Adobe City until Lott got the necessary answers back from the wires he had sent east.

Despite the confidence he had shown in Mike DeWitt, Ridge was still a little worried about what might happen if the miner went back to his old ways, got drunk, and then started spreading the news around town that a marshal had arrived to investigate the robberies. That could place Ridge in a very dangerous position.

But Parkman instinctively believed he had made the right decision in picking DeWitt, and he had learned over the years that, more often than not, his hunches and instinctive choices proved to be correct. It was done now, and he was not going to waste much time worrying about it until something happened to make him worry.

As far as his search for the outlaws was concerned, he had very little to go on except a few guesses and some logical assumptions from what he had heard and seen since beginning this case.

First, he knew there were quite a few outlaws in the band, as many as thirty according to the wagon guards he had talked with. That meant they probably had a fairly large, established main camp, and the camp would have to be in a place where every fortune-hungry rock cracker was not about to stumble across it. But it had to be within a reasonable distance of town, too, probably not more than a day's ride out. That distance in a circle around DeWitt's Strike took in a lot of rugged, mountainous territory.

About an hour's ride north of town, Ridge

took to the hills, deliberately seeking out the thickly forested slopes where most prospectors would not be likely to go. Any prospector who knew his business would stick to the valleys where creeks and streams could be panned and sluiced, and where outcroppings of rock could be checked for deposits of gold-bearing ore.

He rode all day without stopping as he worked his way north through the rough country on a route approximately parallel to the valley trail. By nightfall he had traveled only about ten miles from town because of the meandering, zigzag course he had chosen.

He camped that night in the thick forest, building a fire only large enough to boil a pot of coffee and heat a can of beans for supper. After the simple meal, he built himself a smoke and savored a last cup of coffee before dousing the coals of the fire and settling down between his blankets on the thick mat of pine needles.

The first rays of sunlight roused him the next morning, and after a hasty breakfast he packed up and was on his way again.

The second day was more or less a repetition of the first. He continued his slow progress north, crisscrossing the mountain slopes and valleys. By late afternoon he had started due west, deciding to go back to the main valley before nightfall.

Murky dusk was just beginning to fall when he reached the main valley and began picking up the landmarks his miner friends had given him to reach their claim. He found the elbow bend in the stream and the ruins of a burned-out cabin beyond, and turned due east as Abe had instructed.

The quickly approaching darkness made the riding difficult on the moonless night, but he had the wagon ruts to follow as he made his way along the winding rock path up the mountainside. He was not sure exactly how far ahead the claim was, but Abe had told him that this trail led directly to their mine.

Ridge heard the crack of a rifle shot not too far ahead, and a bullet whacked a rock near him and went singing away into the night. The marksman had apparently fired at the sound of Bill's hooves on the stones and the bullet had not hit very close to Ridge, but he still stepped to the ground and waited quietly, gun in hand, to see what would happen next.

"Jes' hold on right there," a voice said from somewhere in the rocks above, "an' tell me who you are."

"It's Ridge Parkman, Abe," Ridge called

out. "Hold off on that lead slingin' up there."

"Come on up, Ridge," Abe called out. "I ain't a'goin' to shoot you, boy."

Ridge stayed on foot, picking his way up the hillside and leading Bill. Within a hundred yards he reached a small level area and paused. Directly in front of him, nestled against a sheer wall of rock, was a tiny cabin, recognizable only by the dark color of its log walls against the lighter shade of the stone beyond. Ten feet to one side of the cabin was an even darker void, the gaping mouth of their Pipe Dream Mine.

Abe appeared from out of the darkness to one side of Ridge, rifle in hand, and a moment later Dolf and Oak made their presence known, one coming out of the mine and the other standing up from behind a small stone wall near the cabin.

"That was a downright unfriendly welcome," Ridge drawled as he turned to shake Abe's hand.

"We've got that way, a'right," Abe allowed. "But you might give a body some warnin' before you jus' come sashayin' up like that."

"Wal, I didn't know how close I was, or even whether I was at the right place a'tall." He turned and greeted Dolf and Oak as they came walking over from the direction of the cabin.

"We've got so we're jittery as crickets on a hot griddle," Abe said.

"It's why we're still alive," Dolf added.

As the four of them turned and started toward the darkened cabin, Ridge asked, "More trouble, huh?"

"Not us," Dolf said, "but a drifter come through here a day or so ago an' said he found a dead man at the next claim down. It was a friend of ours, Peter Bolton. They dropped him stone dead with a bullet in the gut at the mouth of his mine."

"Yeh, dammit, I told ol' Pete he better get hisself a pardner down there to help him look out after things," Abe said, "but he wasn't havin' no part of sharin' his strike with nobody."

"So now he's shared it all," Dolf added bitterly.

When they got inside the cabin, Abe waited to light the kerosene lamp until Dolf and Oak carefully covered the two small windows with blankets.

The interior of the twelve-by-twelve log cabin was jammed with equipment and the few household furnishings of the three men. A table and four crude wooden chairs filled the center of the room. One wall was stacked from floor to ceiling with the provisions and equipment which they had bought a few days earlier in town. In the back of the cabin was a stove and cooking equipment, and along the other side wall were the men's bunks. The door was in the center of the front wall, with a window cut through the logs on each side of it. Below the windows, several rifle slots were cut through the walls, and the front portion of the cabin was kept clear so the men inside could move around easily during a fight.

As the four of them settled down around the table, Abe said with a wide grin, "Wal, fellers, I 'spect this is enough of an occasion to break out the bottle for a little snort."

"Might as well," Dolf grumbled, " 'fore you have it all drunk up snitchin' gulps when you think nobody's lookin'."

Abe mumbled some sort of sheepish explanation as he got the bottle and four tin cups from the shelves beside the stove. As he poured the liquor into the cups, he asked, "What brings you up our way, Ridge?"

"The gold bug, I guess," Ridge said. "I tried a shotgun job for the freight company, but I decided dyin' young didn't suit me. I figgered to do some scoutin' around an' see if there wasn't a little gold layin' around somewhere for me."

"You made a run on the freight wagons?" Abe asked incredulously. "What in tarnation would make a sensible man like you do such a danged fool thing?"

"A hundred dollars did it," Ridge lied. "But one time was enough to teach me better. They hit us quicker'n rattlers. Killed five men an' got away with every ounce we was haulin'. Even took my horse an' my outfit. The whole shebang."

"That's too bad, but hell, boy, you shoulda knowed better."

"Yeh, I ain't smart like you fellers," Ridge teased. "Sittin' out here in the middle of the wilderness waitin' to be picked off like gophers."

"We have good reasons to need the gold we dig for," Oak said quietly. He had been silent since Ridge's arrival and it was surprising to hear him speak up now.

"It's a fact," Abe said. "Course no man scarcely ever has no objections to gettin' rich, but there is some things that'll make even a sensible man take a few more risks. Like ol' Oak here wantin' to help out his Cherokee people down in Oklahomie, or Dolf here wantin' to get his family out of the coal mines in Pennsylvania an' bring 'em out west here where they can make a new start. Them's fine reasons.

"Me, I guess I got the worst reason of all," Abe went on. "I been trekkin' these mountains, man an' boy, for near fifty years, trappin', tradin', fightin', an' killin' jus' to stay alive. Now I'm old an' tired. I jus' like the idee of maybe layin' back on my duff for my last couple or three years an' goin' out in a bed with sheets on it 'stead of out in the mountains somewhere where don't nobody even know I passed."

"Even if it ain't much," Dolf added, "we've earned what we got an' we'll fight to keep it."

"Any man would," Ridge agreed quietly.

After a while Oak rose and got his rifle from the rack beside the door. "Someone should guard," he said. Abe put out the lamp until the Indian had eased out the door on silent moccasined feet, then relit it and poured another swallow of the precious liquor for Ridge, Dolf, and himself.

Ridge was soon into a blow-by-blow description of the trip down to Adobe City and the well-planned ambush in Bloody Run. The other two men listened intently, showing their anger with occasional muttered curses and condemnations of the outlaws.

When he had finished, Dolf said, "And still after a thing like that the government won't send us any help?"

"Joe McKinney, the trail boss, checked with the law down there," Ridge said, "but it seems like they're long on problems an' short on men here in Colorado. The army's pulled a lot of men out of the garrison in Adobe City an' sent 'em up to fight Sioux north of here, an' the marshals are jus' spread too thin."

"Still seems like they could be doin' somethin' for us," Abe said.

"What I don't understand is why the folks round these parts hadn't tried to do nothin' for themselves," Ridge said. "Other places I been, the folks gen'rally already have some leaders an' lawmen picked by the time their town's this old. They don't always jus' sit around like a bunch of sheep to get picked off one by one."

"Folks is all too busy diggin' for gold an' tryin' to get rich, I reckon," Abe said.

"Ain't doin' 'em much good, though," Ridge said. "Like your friend Bolton. I s'pect he'd give up all the gold he'd ever seen in his life jus' to be alive again."

Abe gave Ridge a curious glance and asked, "Where'd you say you was headed, Ridge?"

"Out prospectin'."

"By your own self?"

"Yeh," Ridge admitted, chuckling as he understood the point of the questions.

"So shut up with all the moralizin', boy. You're jus' as greedy, as the rest of us."

"Maybe," Ridge said, wishing suddenly that he could tell them the real reason he was there. But he felt that the time was not yet right for that revelation; maybe soon, but not yet.

Ridge Parkman's careful search of the countryside around DeWitt's Strike took most of the next four days, but his efforts were fruitless. He found nothing that gave him any hint of where the outlaw band might be hiding.

After leaving the mine of his three friends, he had made a wide sweep in a circle around the town, riding a few miles north, then traveling west until he was in the rugged mountains on the opposite side of the valley. Finally he turned south again in the general direction of DeWitt's Strike.

In time he ended up back in the vicinity of Bloody Run. He scouted around until he found the exact location of the deadly pass. Making a wide sweep around one end, he descended from the ragged heights above and came at last to the lower end of the pass.

An eerie, whining breeze was blowing

down between the steep walls of stone, as if the spirits of the men who had died there lingered on, moaning for revenge. The sound of Bill's hooves on the stones clattered like the rattle of dry bones, and despite the early afternoon heat, Ridge felt a clammy coolness settle over him.

But despite the morbid tension of the place and the distinct sensation of impending violence and danger, Ridge forced himself to remain calm. He was here looking for clues, for any hints that might eventually lead him to the outlaws. When he reached the place where the ambush on the wagons had taken place, he dismounted and went ahead on foot, leading Bill and looking closely at the canyon floor and the steep walls above.

There was not much to be found there. Even the bloodstains on the ground where his fellow guards had died were already gone.

Spotting the place where the explosive charge had been set in a fault in the rocks, Ridge looked the area over closely and decided that the explosives must have been lowered on a rope from the rocks above, or else lit and tossed down into some wide crack where it would blow large amounts of rock down on the unfortunate men who happened to be in the pass at the time.

He felt a definite sense of relief as he mounted Bill and rode out the opposite end of the canyon. But he was not finished yet. He scouted around until he found a narrow trail which led up to the ledges above the pass.

He was searching for a good hiding place, some vantage point where he might hide and witness the attack on the next shipment of gold. If he couldn't make any progress by being a part of the troop of guards, he thought then he might be able to learn something by just laying back and watching it all happen. It was a morbid thought, hiding and watching as men fought for their lives, but it might be the only way.

The ledge above the pass was slashed with a series of faults and cracks running down the rock wall, some several feet wide and others so narrow that a man could barely squeeze down into them. There was a trail of sorts, probably dating back to the days when Indians were the only men who traveled these mountains, which ran the full length of the ledge.

Before it got too dark to find the winding trail down, Ridge turned Bill around and headed back down to the wide grassy meadow that funneled into the entrance of

Bloody Run.

He camped that night in a thick clump of cottonwoods on one edge of the meadow, and by the light of his tiny campfire, he began working out a plan.

CHAPTER 8

When Ridge arrived back in DeWitt's Strike, he dropped off his horse and gear at Gomez's corrals. The hostler was not there so Ridge started off into town to find Mike DeWitt. He had been gone for nearly a week now, which was plenty of time for DeWitt to have made it down to Adobe City and back — provided DeWitt had not fallen back into a whiskey bottle somewhere.

He walked the town from end to end, stopping in a few of the saloons, but De-Witt was not in any of them. Along the way he also stopped at the small shed behind the Last Nuggett where DeWitt had slept when he worked in the saloon, but De-Witt's bedroll was not there either.

Finally he stopped in a saloon and bought himself a bottle, then headed back to the corrals to have a drink with Gomez. He figured that if DeWitt was back or came back any time soon, he would eventually check there to try and locate Ridge.

Gomez was back at the corrals when Ridge arrived, shoveling hay over into the pens for the thirty or so horses inside. As he walked past the Mexican, Ridge showed him the bottle and said, "Let's go inside an' have a drink, amigo. I been out for a week now an' I'm plumb dry." Gomez needed no persuading to share the bottle.

Inside the shed Ridge took two cups to the table and filled each to the brim. Gomez took a large gulp of the firewater, showed his appreciation with a wide grin, and said, "Senor DeWitt came here to see you yesterday, but I told him you were out looking for gold and so he left again."

"What did he say?" Ridge asked. "Did he tell you where he was going or say he'd come back later?"

"Yes, senor. He said to tell you that he was going to his mine and that you could find him there when you returned."

"Where is his mine, Gomez?"

"It is close, senor. The closest mine to town, and the most worthless. Come outside and I will show you."

They stepped to the door of the shed and Gomez, squinting into the morning sun, pointed to a dark mine entrance about a quarter of a mile away and midway up the nearest steep mountainside. "That is the hole in the ground, Senor Ridge, which started all this madness here. That is the DeWitt's Strike Mine."

They went back inside to finish their drinks, but Ridge gulped his down quickly, in a hurry to go up and find out what information DeWitt had brought back from Henry Lott in Adobe City. In a few minutes he left Gomez sitting with the bottle to keep him company and started on foot toward the mine.

He waded the small river easily. The water was down today, but in the short time Ridge had been here he had seen the water level rise and fall several times and knew that the next rainfall would again turn the trickle of water into a torrent.

It was a short climb up the side of the hill to the mine. A couple of hundred feet from the entrance he rounded the slag pile of rock which DeWitt had dug out of his shaft and came to the mouth of the hole itself. About ten feet back into the mine, shores had been wedged in between the floor and ceiling and boards were nailed up to completely block access to the remainder of the tunnel. The word "Danger" was painted prominently across the boards, and below in smaller letters the message read, "This

114

mine ain't safe."

Looking the barrier over closely, Ridge saw that a couple of boards on one side had been pulled loose and hung only by one nail each at the top. He pushed one of the boards aside and peered inside. Once his eyes had adjusted to the dimness, he saw a faint glow back around the first bend of the shaft.

"Hey! Mike DeWitt! You in there?" he called out. "It's Ridge Parkman."

"Yeh, Ridge," a voice answered from back in the shaft. "Hold on a minute an' I'll come up there."

Ridge pushed the boards further aside and stepped inside. The cool, moist air in the mine smelled faintly of rock dust and wood smoke. He waited as a light began bobbing down the shaft toward him.

In a moment DeWitt appeared, carrying a battered kerosene lamp in one hand. Even in the flickering lamplight, Ridge could tell that DeWitt was clear-eyed and alert, and he noticed that the miner had even shaved recently.

"You know," Mike said, stopping near Ridge, "I ain't been in this here mine in two, maybe three, months, but somebody has. Them boards was popped when I come up, an' I found some burnt up matches right there where you're standin'."

"Why would anybody want to come in here?" Ridge asked. "Didn't you say the gold was played out?"

"Shore is, an' besides that, I got some split shoring on toward the back. Ain't safe to go back there a'tall. Ain't no tellin' when half this durned mountain might come tumblin' down."

"Musta been drifters or somebody that couldn't afford the price of a bed in town," Ridge said, dismissing the subject. He was more interested in getting the news from Adobe City. "Did you see Henry Lott?"

"Yeh, I seen him," DeWitt said. "He give me a letter to give you. Come on. It's back here."

As Ridge followed the older miner back into the shaft, he eyed all the shoring and supports warily, mindful of what DeWitt had said a moment earlier. But DeWitt explained that the only danger in the mine was toward the back and that he did not intend to go back that far.

About fifty yards in they came to an area where the walls of the tunnel widened out to perhaps fifteen feet across and the ceiling rose to a height of ten feet.

"I hit the richest part of the vein right here," DeWitt said with a trace of sadness in his voice. "It branched out in three places and went all which-away. I got twelve maybe fifteen hundred dollars' worth outa just this one place."

To one side of the chamber DeWitt had set up his meager household. His blankets were spread out in a level place, and nearby were the cold ashes of a fire. Beside the ashes were a couple of empty cans and a few sticks of wood.

DeWitt reached into a crack in the rock near his bedroll and pulled out an envelope. As he handed it to Ridge, he said proudly, "I ain't opened it. That feller Lott said it was jus' for you to see an' nobody else."

"Thanks, Mike." Ridge took the envelope from DeWitt and tore it open. By the lamplight he carefully read the three pages of information Lott had sent, then reread them once again.

Henry Lott had been busy in the few days since Ridge had been in Adobe City. His letter contained quite a bit of information.

He began with what he had found out about Herbert Reynolds from sources in the east. Reynolds, he said, was apparently the same Herbert Reynolds who had been involved in a major banking scandal in Philadelphia about six months before. Soon after government agents began an investiga-

117

tion into the embezzlement of nearly a quarter of a million dollars from a banking system there, Reynolds, a key suspect at the time, had disappeared. At the time it was believed that Reynolds had taken some or all of the stolen money with him and that his leaving was equivalent to an admission of guilt.

However, as the investigation progressed, it was becoming more likely that some of Reynolds's associates had covered up their own guilt by making evidence point to Reynolds and that he had disappeared so he would not be tried and punished for crimes he did not commit.

The government, Lott wrote, is very interested in finding out where Herbert Reynolds is now.

The information about Bramwell was more tentative, but it did provide Ridge with some interesting material for speculation. Bramwell, it seemed, fit almost identically the description of a man named Jack "Slickie" Kirk, who had been run out of the gold and silver fields of California a couple of years before.

Kirk had operated a saloon, casino, and brothel there, and was suspected of running crooked games and of causing the deaths of occasional wealthy miners who sought the attentions of the girls in his employment. But when it was learned that he was the front man for an outlaw band that had been victimizing the local miners, irate local residents burned his business to the ground. Kirk narrowly escaped the angry mob by dressing up like a woman and fleeing the burning building with his girls. Then he had disappeared.

Lott said he had a deputy who had been in California goldfields at about the time Kirk was there and that as soon as the lawman could be called in he would be sent to make a positive identification of Bramwell as Kirk.

Lott had been unable to dig up much information about Joe McKinney except that he had served in the Union Army from 1862 to 1866.

When Ridge finished his second reading of the letter he folded it back into its envelope and put it in his pocket.

"Good stuff?" DeWitt asked, noticing Ridge's satisfied smile.

"I reckon so," Ridge said. "It helps a lot to know some 'bout the people we're dealin' with."

"Wal, I still wanta help, Ridge," DeWitt assured him eagerly. "Ridin' down there an' bringin' that letter back to you, wal, it felt

119

right good to be useful for somethin' again, an' not jus' bein' a no-count drunk wallowin' around the gutters an' scrubbin' out spittoons. You kin count on me right down the line 'til you catch them hombres."

"Okay, Mike," Ridge said, reaching out and shaking the other man's hand. "I will count on you, an' I will use you. 'Fore this thing is finished, I'll be needin' every bit of help I can round up anywhere. But right now let's just go get us somethin' to eat. How about it?"

Ridge was silent during much of the meal and DeWitt just let him alone, knowing the deputy marshal was mulling over the information from the letter and deciding what they should do next.

After the meal, over coffee, Ridge finally seemed ready to begin discussing a plan. "How much trouble would it be," he began tentatively, "to find out when the next shipment of gold was goin' out?"

"It's s'posed to be kept secret," DeWitt said, "but sometimes word gets out an' a few folks know ahead when they're gettin' ready to leave. They's ways to tell, like when they start callin' in the men, or when the water barrels get filled an' the horses get extra special care an' feed the night before."

"To do what I want to do, we're goin' to have to know ahead of time when the next shipment will leave."

DeWitt thought a moment, then said, "It'll take a lot of watchin' an' snoopin' around, but I think I could handle it." He considered it a moment longer, then added, "But I don't see what good it'll do you. Ain't no one man, marshal or not, goin' to stop that bunch of thugs from doin' what they want to. You done tried that one time, ain't you?"

"No sir, that shore didn't work," Ridge agreed. "But this time I wouldn't try to stop 'em. I'd jus' lay back somewhere an' watch it all happen without even raisin' a finger."

"An' then follow 'em to see where they go," DeWitt said, understanding at last.

"Somethin' like that. Seems to me that somehow they always know what's goin' on here an' when to hit, an' nobody ever knows who they are or where they run to hide when the shootin's over. What we gotta do is turn the tables on 'em one time."

"I shore would love to be there to see that," DeWitt said with a grin. "I shore would."

"We'll see what we can do," Ridge told him. "But right now we gotta think about right now. You get out an' keep your ear to the ground. Me, I'm gonna get ready to do some serious trackin'."

"That might be a big problem, Ridge. You ever tried to track acrost these rocks an' mountains an' gullies? Why, a man's gotta mite near be an Injun to do it."

Ridge sat back, drawing deeply on his cigarette and smiling as he let the smoke blow back out between his lips. "You're thinkin' right, Mike. An Indian could do it"

CHAPTER 9

For the second time in less than a week, Ridge made the ride out to the Pipe Dream Mine to see his three allies there, but on this trip he timed his arrival so he would get there during the daytime. Starting from town at dawn, he reached the mine in mid-afternoon.

As he rode up through the rocks toward the shaft, Oak appeared from a concealed spot near the wagon trail and greeted him. "Our friend is back," the Indian said.

"Yeh," Ridge said. "I got some business in mind I think you fellers'll be interested in. Where's Abe an' the Dutchman?"

As if in answer to his question, the two miners came trotting out of the mine entrance and across the open area outside where they stopped and looked back toward the shaft. A moment later the ground shook as the roar of an explosive blast rolled out from inside the mine. Within seconds, thick clouds of rock dust rolled out the mine entrance and the two miners settled down on some rocks to let the dust settle before they started back in.

"I see you boys is still makin' holes in that mountain," Ridge called out as he rode over toward them.

With a grin on his dust-blackened face, Abe said, "Shore are. An' this blast might be our fortune, too. From all we can tell, that little vein we been followin' has turned straight down an' started to widen out. This could be it."

"Maybe," Dolf said cynically. "But we've thought that before. Remember?"

"Cheer up, boy," Abe said good-naturedly. "Jus' think. If we started blastin' more, 'fore too long you'd have to make a trip into town to buy more dynamite from that purty little gal's daddy down there. Might even get the chance to get your face whanged up for her again."

"When we make our strike, then we can start thinkin' about women," Dolf grumbled, but it was plain that the mention of Marjorie Reynolds had struck a special note in him.

"What brings you back up here, Ridge?" Abe asked. "Jus' can't get enough of our charmin' comp'ny?"

"That's not exac'ly it," Ridge grinned. "I got sort of a proposition to see if you three fellers are interested in. Let's go up to your cabin an' parley. You too, Oak," he said to the Indian.

When the four of them were settled around the table in the cabin, without ceremony Ridge pulled out his badge and dropped it on the table in front of them. The three of them stared at the badge a moment and then looked up at Ridge, not yet understanding what this was all about.

"Where'd you get that?" Abe asked. "Did you find a dead marshal somewheres . . . or kill one?"

"It's mine," Ridge said. "I'm a deputy marshal. I've been sent over here from Denver to see if I can't put a stop to some of this trouble."

"I'm glad the government thought enough of us to send such a large force," Dolf said with a frown.

"What one man can do sometimes depends on the man," Ridge said simply.

"Yeh, I reckon you're so tough," Abe chuckled, "alls you got to do is jus' ride in an' tell the raiders they're all under arrest. Hell, there ain't but thirty or forty of 'em. You can get the drop on 'em easy."

"I don't 'spect I'll be tryin' nothin' like

that," Ridge said, "but I do have a plan if you two'll quit flappin' your jaws long enough to hear about it. Won't cost nothin' to listen 'cept time."

"We got plenty of time," Dolf said. "Can't get back in that mine for a couple of hours or better 'til that rock dust clears."

Ridge picked up the badge and put it back in his pocket, then began outlining what he had in mind. "I can get the help I need when the time comes," he said, "from the army garrison in Adobe City, but they won't send no soldiers to wander around these hills on no fishin' trips.

"What I have to do is find out where them raiders hole up, an' to do that I need me a tracker. I need a man that can track jus' like he was an Indian or somethin'."

He paused and Abe said, "Well, Ridge, we got Oak here, an' he's . . ." Then he understood. "That's why you come, ain't it?"

Ridge turned to the Indian and asked, "How about it, Oak? Could you handle the job?"

"I can follow men by the signs they leave on the ground," Oak said quietly. "I will help you."

"Good," Ridge said, smiling his satisfaction. "Now, as for the other two of you, I need you, too. I want to set up a watch on that freight office in town twenty-four hours a day. I want to know every man that comes or goes from there between now an' the next time a shipment of gold leaves out of there. Shouldn't take more than a week or two an' I can pay you gov'ment wages 'til the job's done. Should mean ten or fifteen dollars apiece for you."

"Hell, we'd do it for free if it meant puttin' a stop to all this killin' an' robbin'," Abe said. "Don't forget, 'fore too long we're hopin' that some of that gold goin' down to the banks in Adobe City will be ours."

"Okay, it's settled, then," Ridge said. "We'll leave as soon as you can hitch your team."

Night fell when they were little more than halfway to town, but Ridge insisted that they push on through the darkness and get there as soon as possible. His entire plan depended upon being there when the next shipment of gold went down, and he did not want to waste even a single night and risk the chance of missing it.

When they reached the edge of town, Ridge led them directly up to the DeWitt's Strike Mine. He had decided to make that his base of operations, both because it was a short distance out of town and because the back door and loading platform of the freight office were in plain view of the mine entrance. He and his allies could sit up there and watch every move that was made behind that building. If anybody inquired about the sudden new activity at the mine, Ridge had already agreed that DeWitt would tell people he was thinking about reopening the mine and giving it another try.

When they reached the mine, Ridge had Dolf take the wagon and horses to Gomez's corrals. He next set the men up on a schedule to keep a constant watch on the freight office. For the next couple of nights the full moon would provide plenty of light to see if any wagon train was being assembled in the staging area behind the freight office, and after that they would have to find a hidden vantage point on down the hillside to watch from.

When everything was settled at the mine, Ridge walked down into town to find De-Witt. That might take some time, he decided, because the town was still very much alive with its usual boisterous nighttime frenzy. He started down one side of the street, working his way through the crowds of rowdy, staggering drunks and stepping cautiously into doorways or around the sides of buildings each time he heard the crack of gunfire.

When he finally spotted Mike DeWitt, his spirits dropped and a burst of anger flooded through him. The miner was sitting in the dust, slumped against the wall of a saloon in the middle of town. His head was sagging over sideways, as if he had passed out in a drunken stupor, and an empty whiskey bottle lay on the ground beside him, inches away from his splayed fingers.

Ridge resisted the urge to kick DeWitt. Instead he stooped beside him and shook him roughly. "Dammit, Mike, you drunken bastard," he said.

DeWitt raised his head and looked at Ridge. "Get outa here an' leave me alone," he said in a cautious voice which showed no hint of drunkenness. "I'm watchin', Ridge, an' I thought this would be the best way to go about it."

Ridge glanced back across his shoulder and saw that from where DeWitt sat, he had a clear view of the front and one side of the freight office across the street. "Sorry, pardner," he chuckled. "I thought you'd fell off the wagon on me."

DeWitt waited until a couple of drinkers had staggered by, and then said, "I promised I wouldn't let you down an' I won't. I figgered wouldn't nobody pay me no mind if I jus' acted the way I been actin' all the time.

I can stay here all night if I'm of a mind, an' won't nobody give me a second look."

"Okay, Mike," Ridge said. "I'll be at the mine if you need to find me. I've got some friends up there, too. Them three miners I was tellin' you 'bout."

As he stood up to leave, DeWitt wiggled around to a more comfortable position and let his head settle back onto his shoulder, his eyes almost closed, but watching.

CHAPTER 10

Ridge woke with Abe kneeling above him, shaking his shoulder. He blinked his eyes and looked up at the excited face of the miner in the dim lamplight inside the mine.

"Pay dirt, Ridge," Abe said. "They started bringin' horses round to the back of the freight office an' hitchin' 'em up to the wagons."

Ridge sat up and began pulling on his boots. He had slept with his clothes on and had only to get up, strap on his gun, and put on his hat to be ready to leave. Nearby, both Oak and Dolf were sitting up, roused by Abe's words.

Ridge was glad that the time had finally come. They had been watching the freight office in shifts for three days now and the time was beginning to drag as they waited for another wagon train to be put together. As Ridge was checking his rifle and getting his saddlebags, Oak was also up and preparing to leave.

At the entrance to the mine they met Mike DeWitt coming in. "You saw, huh?" he asked as he stepped through the opening in the boards.

"Yeh, I guess this is it," Ridge said. Before he and Oak went out to carry out their part of the plan, he gave some final instructions to DeWitt, Abe, and Dolf, who were all going to stay behind. "Don't forget now, when we get gone, you keep a close lookout for anybody that might be leavin' the freight office in a hurry. Watch Bramwell an' Reynolds. We need to know where they go to round town an' who they talk to. I don't 'spect either one'll leave town right after the wagons 'cause that'd be too obvious, but one of them might have a messenger he can send out to get word to the outlaws. An' be careful. This is a powerful serious game here an' if they was to find out what we've been doin' they wouldn't mind a'tall puttin' bullets in the lot of us."

"Jus' you an' Oak watch out for your own tails, too, marshal," Abe warned. "You're the ones that's got the hardest job ahead of you."

They shook hands around and Ridge and Oak left the mine. As they started down the hill toward the corrals, the first pink and

orange beginnings of dawn were just starting to appear over the mountain peaks to
the east.

They made their way quickly to the corrals and began hitching two horses to the
wagon. Ridge knew that two horsemen riding south out of town shortly before a gold
shipment started out in that direction would
be too obvious a move, so he had decided
that he and Oak would leave going north in
the wagon. After they hitched up the team,
they got two saddles from the shed and hid
them under a canvas in the back of the
wagon. The sleepy and still half-drunk
Gomez watched all of this with a measure
of curiosity until Ridge explained that he
and the Indian were going to return the
wagon to the Pipe Dream Mine and then
go out prospecting further north on horseback. As they climbed up onto the wagon
seat, the Mexican staggered back toward
the shed and his waiting bed.

The main street was deserted and nobody
seemed to note their passing as they drove
north through town and on up the wagon
trail. Ridge drove on for about half an hour
before choosing a grove of trees far off the
trail as a likely place to leave the wagon.
When it was stopped and out of sight of the
trail, Ridge and Oak unharnessed the horses

and saddled them.

They rode quickly but cautiously in the growing dawn, skirting wide around De-Witt's Strike as they headed back south. Ridge figured that by now the wagons had probably already left town, but his and Oak's progress on horseback would be much faster than that of the heavy freight wagons and he was sure they would have no trouble getting far ahead of them before they reached ambush country.

But he also had to think about running into the band of outlaws as they assembled to hit the wagons. He was only betting that this ambush would take place in Bloody Run as so many had before, but if he bet wrong, he knew that it could be disastrous for him and his Indian scout.

By midmorning they had ridden through the first few potential ambush areas, and their luck was holding out. They had not seen anybody since they left town. As they got closer to the meadow above Bloody Run, Ridge slowed their pace and he and Oak began watching closely for any signs that they were being watched.

Then at last they reached the small meadow above the deadly pass. This was going to be one of the trickiest parts of the whole operation, Ridge knew. They had to cross the open areas where they would be easy targets for anybody who might decide their presence was not wanted.

Telling Oak to hold back out of sight for a while, Ridge rode cautiously to about midway down the meadow and then turned left toward the cottonwood grove where he had camped when he was here a few days before. When he reached the grove safely and was out of sight in the trees, Oak traced his path until he had joined Ridge in the trees.

They tied the horses far back into the trees where nobody on the trail could possibly spot them, then started out on foot. It was easier to slip around on foot, but their progress was slow as they worked their way down the edge of the meadow to the twisting, rocky trail that led to the ledges above Bloody Run. Ridge guessed that by the time they reached the top, they were no more than a couple of hours ahead of the wagons, provided that none of the wagons stopped as the one on the last trip had. And still they had yet to see the first sign of an outlaw.

It would be ironic, Ridge thought, if this was the first gold shipment in nearly three months that made it through to Adobe City without being attacked. He had to admit that it would be a pleasure to see the wagons pass peacefully from one end of Bloody Run to the other, but it would also delay his entire plan and he and Oak would have no choice but to go back to DeWitt's Strike and continue the wait until another gold shipment was sent out.

They reached the center of the ledge and found themselves a secluded spot where they could watch whatever went on far below them. It was a good location, a jagged crack in the rock with enough of an overhanging ledge to hide them from anybody who might pass along above them, and plenty of cover in front so they would not be easily spotted from across the pass. Ridge settled down toward the back of the niche with his rifle and canteen, and Oak stayed closer to the front to watch.

They had been there only about twenty minutes when Oak called back to Ridge in a calm, hushed voice, "They have come." Ridge stayed still, only moving his head slightly to see Oak ease back to better cover and hunker down against the rocks.

Ridge could see no movement from where he was sitting, but in a few minutes he began hearing occasional voices that seemed to be coming from the ledge on the other side of the pass. Once he glimpsed a man slipping across the rocks on that side, but the man did not turn his gaze in the right direction to spot Ridge and Oak. He was soon out of sight.

In another few minutes all the outlaws had picked their positions, and quiet again settled over the pass and the ledges above. Only the occasional whoosh and whine of the wind rushing through the pass broke the tense stillness which engulfed Bloody Run. Oak eased cautiously toward the front of the crack, moving so slowly that it took him several minutes to cover no more than eight feet. He stayed there a short while, then eased back to Ridge again.

"I can see four on the rocks across the pass," he whispered to Ridge, "but there are probably more."

"Yeh, they'll have snipers and maybe an explosives man up there," Ridge said, "but the main bunch will be down below at one end of the pass or the other. I jus' hope they don't decide to hide out in those same trees where our horses are tied."

Oak nodded his agreement, then turned and moved partway back to the front.

The slow minutes of waiting stretched into more than an hour before there was any sign of the wagons. Finally Oak turned his head slowly back toward Ridge and pointed with a finger toward the head of the pass. A moment later Ridge heard the first clatter of iron wheel rims and horses' hooves on the rocky trail.

Sitting hunkered down in the fissure of rock, Ridge listened to the increasing noise below as the wagons neared, and considered the lunacy of this gold business. Down below him there was maybe twenty men, some of whom would soon die defending a load of soft yellow metal in a wagon, and in the rocks around him were other men who were all quite willing to kill just to put some of that same metal in their pockets. It seemed crazy that men would place more value on that stuff than they would on human life.

But before his scorn grew too great, he realized that gold had brought him here, too. The only reason he was there now, sweating in a tight little crack in the side of the mountain, was to make it possible for men to get their yellow metal from one place to another safely.

It was a truly crazy business.

His thoughts were drawn back to the situation at hand by the same startling howl which he had heard before when he was a guard down there in the pass. It was some sort of signal for the outlaws, Ridge decided.

Then came the deafening explosion which

sent another barrage of rock crashing down on the men and animals below. Before the earth quit trembling from the explosion, rifles were already cracking, picking off the guards and drivers.

The gunfire momentarily rose in intensity and was soon joined by the rumble of horses' hooves as the main band of outlaws rode into the pass to complete the capture. Ridge did not bother to move forward to watch. He had seen men die before and the sight of it held no fascination for him.

Within a couple of minutes the gunfire died down to only a few occasional shots and then finally ceased. Ridge moved forward cautiously to Oak's side. Below them and a short distance down the pass about twenty-five mounted raiders were just rounding up the surviving wagon guards and drivers. The bodies of half a dozen men were sprawled randomly about the battlefield and three horses lay dead in their traces.

As Ridge and the Indian watched, some of the raiders quickly transferred the small cases of gold from a wagon bed to packs on three waiting mules. Other outlaws were rounding up the surviving horses and going through the pockets of the captured men.

Within ten minutes of the last shot, the

band of raiders were mounted up and thundering away down the narrow pass.

"Jus' bam, bam, grab the gold an' hightail it," Ridge muttered to Oak. "Quick as a snake an' neat as a pin. The bastards."

Ridge and Oak waited only long enough for the outlaws across the path to leave before they climbed up out of their hiding place and started back along the ledge. Ridge saw no need to wait around and watch the survivors of the attack gather up their dead and wounded. He knew the routine.

They took their time retrieving their horses from the grove of trees in the meadow. Not only did they have to wait for the wagons to clear out of the pass before they could get through, but they had no urge to follow along too closely after the outlaw band. If the raiders were as smart about their escape as they had been about the attack, they might leave a rear guard behind to discourage pursuit.

In the cottonwood grove Ridge and Oak ate some jerky and hardtack from their saddlebags, then settled back to pass an hour or so before they proceeded with their mission. The two had very little to say to each other; with the Indian such silence was customary, but the echoing sights and sounds of death accounted for Ridge Parkman's very unaccustomed quietness.

When the afternoon sun was midway down the western sky, Ridge decided that they should leave. He estimated that they would have four or five more hours of daylight to track the outlaws. That would be enough time to get them headed in the right direction, but he was sure that they would have to stop for the night and then pick up the cold trail in the morning. Even an expert tracker had trouble following a trail at night over rocky terrain like this.

But Ridge was glad he had enlisted Oak's aid for this job. Already the Indian had shown he had a keen eye and good sense in a tense situation. Now, Ridge thought, if he was just a good enough tracker, they might finally start making some progress.

They saddled the horses and rode cautiously down into Bloody Run. They listened closely and checked each twist in the trail before riding around it, but the wagons had gone on by then. As they rode out the lower end of the pass and broke out into open country, they could see the six wagons far off down the trail on their way to Adobe City.

That was where Ridge put the Indian to

work. "Okay, Oak. It's your show now. Lead out."

Oak nodded and turned his horse off the trail almost immediately, his eyes fixed on the ground ahead of them. At first they moved due west at a fairly good pace, riding at a quick walk over a wide expanse of grassland. But when they reached another rocky area, Oak began to dismount occasionally and study the signs before determining a direction.

The trail continued west for more than two hours, which surprised Ridge. He had expected the outlaws to be more deceptive in their escape, laying down false trails and making some attempts to disguise the direction they were headed. This straight trail might indicate overconfidence on the part of the leader of the band. That pleased Ridge. Too much confidence had been the undoing of many a man, and it would make for much easier tracking on this chase.

Oak began having difficulties when they reached the first of the ragged hills to the west of Bloody Run. His problems with detecting the signs were compounded by the fading evening light, and at last he stopped and turned to Ridge.

"The day is gone," he said. "If we go on, maybe we lose the tracks."

"Okay, we'll stop here an' start again in the morning," Ridge said.

They spent the night in a small draw, making a cold camp because of the danger that a campfire might be seen too easily at a distance.

At dawn they were back in the saddle, now following a steep, winding trail up the side of a mountain. They topped the crest and started down the other side, having to ride carefully and occasionally dismount to lead their horses over some particularly treacherous stretches.

At the base of that mountain they turned north, working their way up a twisting, ragged draw. Ridge seldom saw any signs now that this was the direction the raiders had gone, but Oak still kept finding enough to keep them on the trail. Finally, far up the draw, they rode out onto another meadow which seemed completely surrounded by rocky slopes that rose so sharply there was no place for a man on horseback to continue on.

Ridge glanced over at Oak in puzzlement and for the first time had a flash of doubt about the Indian's skills. If they had somehow missed a place where the outlaws had turned off, all this effort might have been in vain. But the Indian's eyes were glancing around the ground near them, an expression of calm determination on his face. He dismounted and walked forward a few steps, then knelt and looked at a mark on the ground. Turning his head to look back at Ridge, he said, "The horses came through here. This stone was chipped."

Staring back at his companion, Ridge decided that he had trusted the man this far and might as well go on trusting him. "So where did they go?" he asked.

"There will be a place through the rocks somewhere," Oak said. "We will find it."

They began riding around the perimeter of the open area and within half an hour had proved the truth of Oak's prediction. There was a way through — a narrow pathway winding into a tangle of boulders and rocky outcroppings. They paused there and Oak pointed to a small struggling bush by the trail. A few strands of horsehair clung to the bush.

"We must leave the horses here until we look up there," Oak said. "Maybe a guard stayed behind in this place."

Ridge nodded his agreement and stepped to the ground, pulling his carbine from the saddle boot.

Slipping cautiously through the rocks, they moved forward a hundred yards or

144

more before Oak stopped and tensed, his hearing tuned to something which Ridge had not yet heard. Then, perhaps twenty or thirty feet ahead, Ridge heard a deep, chesty cough and the sound of a man spitting.

Oak turned his head, pointed to Ridge, and then to the ground. Ridge nodded that he would stay there. The Indian leaned his rifle against a rock, then turned and eased up over a head-high rock on one side of the trail. Ridge listened closely for the next few minutes, but never heard the slightest sound. Finally Oak returned down the middle of the trail and retrieved his rifle. "It was only one man," he said as he started again up the trail.

About fifty yards further, the trail crested and a hidden canyon suddenly opened up below them. Ridge felt a surge of excitement as he saw what lay before them and realized that this was it, the object of their quest.

The canyon was a mile long and about a quarter of a mile wide. Halfway along its length, nestled at the base of a cliff which rose several hundred feet, was a cluster of squat log cabins. Near the cabins three large corrals held at least fifty or sixty horses. Smoke was rising from the chimneys of a couple of the cabins and a few people were in sight outside.

Ridge slapped Oak on the shoulder and said happily, "You did it, pardner. What a helluva tracker you turned out to be!"

For the first time since he had known Oak, Ridge saw a smile cross the Indian's face. It was a fleeting expression which only momentarily turned up the corners of his mouth before disappearing.

CHAPTER 11

The bodies of two dead men lay side by side in a slight depression far off the trail, their throats gaping and bloody from a sudden assault by Oak's deadly blade. One of them was the first guard Oak had eliminated when he and Ridge first discovered this place, and the second was an outlaw who had come up to relieve the first.

Ridge had worried for a while that one or both of the guards might be missed by the men in the camp below, but if they were, nobody down there seemed to want to make the effort to come up and see what was going on. They had apparently gone undetected and unmolested for so long that their security precautions had become lax.

After going back to find a better place to hide their horses, Ridge had rejoined Oak on the hillside above the outlaw camp. He brought his spyglass back with him so he could study the layout of the canyon more closely.

During the hours they had been watching, Ridge and Oak had seen three men saddle up horses and ride out in the opposite direction up the canyon. Since they never returned, Ridge decided there must be another way out up there, and he guessed that maybe that was the way they went to reach DeWitt's Strike. He estimated that the hidden canyon was about a three-hour ride southwest of the mining town.

Oak spent part of the day scouting around on foot. He reported back to Ridge that there were indeed two ways in and out of the canyon, one at each end. That news pleased Ridge. It would make a roundup of the bandits easier and it might be possible, if the surprise was complete, to capture every single one of them. But only two entrances also meant that the canyon was a very defensible place, and if the bandits had any warning they would be able to put up a very effective fight before they were overcome or starved out.

Ridge had also made another discovery which pleased him very much. Using the spyglass, he had studied the livestock in the corrals carefully and had spotted a horse he felt sure was President Grant. At that distance it was impossible to be positive, but the size and markings seemed right.

Toward dark he made his first mention to Oak of an idea that he had been working over in his mind for several hours. It was really a harebrained idea and Ridge knew it, knew better than to jeopardize the whole operation with a scheme so foolish, but he could not seem to completely force the idea out of his head.

"I want to get my horse 'fore we leave outa here," Ridge finally announced to the Indian.

Oak did not speak. He continued to stare out over the canyon with his customary lack of expression.

"I know it's a danged fool notion," Ridge said sheepishly, "but hell, he's a right good horse and it sticks in my craw that they stole him from me."

Oak turned his head and looked at Ridge, his features still void of all expression.

"Ain't you gonna say nothin' about that idea?"

"Are you asking me if you should do this thing or telling me what you will do?" the Indian asked.

"Wal, I'm tellin', I guess."

"Then get your horse," Oak said simply.

As darkness came, Ridge prepared to sneak down and retrieve President Grant from the bandit corral. With all the men down there and the anonymity of darkness, Ridge thought he should be able to just walk up, mount the horse, and ride out without any of the outlaws realizing he was not one of them. He could ride the horse toward the upper end of the canyon as if he were headed toward town, then circle around to the lower pass where Oak would be waiting. If he got even as much as a hundred yards away from their camp, he would be home free.

Before leaving, he gave Oak a note that he had written to Henry Lott and gave him some final instructions.

"If I'm not back in, say, one hour, you take both horses an' hightail it for Adobe City. Find Lott an' give him the note I wrote. Then stick around an' lead the soldiers back to this place. If they can come in from both ends at once an' take these jaspers by surprise, it should be duck soup. I know you can handle it, pardner."

Oak nodded his understanding and put the letter in the back pocket of his trousers. He clasped Ridge's hand firmly for a moment before Ridge turned and started off down toward the outlaw camp.

It was easy enough for Ridge to work his way down near the outlaw camp. He stopped when he got near enough to smell the smoke of the fires inside the cabins and to hear the voices of the men who sat around on the stoops of the buildings smoking, drinking whiskey, and swapping yarns.

After watching for a few minutes, he decided that there were no guards around the outside edge of the camp. Finally he just stood up and began walking toward the camp. He got near enough to be within sight of the cabins, and when he was not challenged or apparently noticed, he veered off to the side and headed for the corrals.

The horses bunched up on the opposite side of the corral as Ridge approached, but his low, urgent whistle brought one animal out into the middle of the pen. A broad grin spread across Ridge's face as he recognized the tall, husky President Grant standing there in the center of the enclosure, wanting to come over but not yet certain about it. "Come on over here, big fella," Ridge said quietly. "It's me all right."

The big horse came straight over to him then, sticking his long neck across the skinned poles and nuzzling Ridge like a gentle pet. "Yeah, I'm glad to see you, too, boy," Ridge said affectionately. "But we ain't got no time for socializin' right now. You gotta haul my skinny hide outa here 'fore

151

these owlhoots realize I ain't no friend of theirs." He took a short rope out of his back pocket and slipped the loop around President Grant's neck, then led him down the fence to the pole gate.

Ridge had slid the top two poles of the gate aside when a gruff voice behind him asked suddenly, "Duff know you're goin' into town this time of night?"

"Yeh, I told him," Ridge said without turning.

He pulled on the rope to lead President Grant out of the corral, but the man came up right behind him and said, "Wal, you know better'n to get one of these stolen horses to ride in on. Somebody in town might recognize him an' then they'd know who you are."

With his back still to the man, Ridge paused for a second and thought. "I spoke up for this one to Duff," he said.

"What the . . . ? Wait a minute, you. Turn around here."

Ridge started a slow turn, then speeded it up into a sudden spin, swinging out his right fist toward where the man's head should be. With a loud "crack" his knuckles collided with the butt of the man's upraised rifle, and an instant later the man swung the rifle butt up in a neat, smooth blow to the side of Ridge's head. He went down like a sack of potatoes.

CHAPTER 12

Ridge was getting mighty tired of staring at the rough log wall a foot in front of his face. His head pounded as if a devil had set up housekeeping inside it, but that pain had to compete with a variety of other aches and agonies in a dozen other places.

Whoever had trussed him up must have had a special knack for causing the maximum of pain and discomfort for a man, short of hanging him, with just a few feet of rope. First of all, the loops around his hands and feet were unnecessarily tight, but if that was not enough by itself, another length of rope linked his hands and feet together and then stretched up in a gagging coil about his neck. Each time he straightened his legs even a fraction of an inch to try to gain some relief from the bone-deep aching in them, it pulled the rope at his throat and choked him. Finally, to complete the outfit, his mouth was stuffed with foul-tasting burlap, held in by his own bandanna knotted around his head. He did not have any immediate hopes of escaping.

When he came to here in one of the cabins some indeterminate time before, his first thoughts were about how surprising it was to still be alive. There had to be some reasons other than mere compassion which had convinced the outlaws to tie him up and keep him prisoner, but he could not figure out what they were. It just made sense that they would have shot him instead.

Once somebody had come into the cabin, but his back was to the room and he was unable to turn over so he could only guess that it had been a woman by the lightness of her step. Whoever it was did not speak and only stayed there for a short while.

Every few minutes Ridge told himself that now he had reached the ultimate in pain and that the hurting could not possibly get any worse, but repeatedly his body kept making a liar out of him. He got to the point after a while where he was almost glad he was gagged so he would not have to listen to his own moaning.

He felt a surge of nervous anticipation when he heard heavy footfalls on the porch outside and the cabin door scraped open. As the steps came into the cabin, a deep male voice said, "Damnation, I hate that! I was sorta lookin' forward to puttin' him away in some kind of stylish way, you know, like the redskins used to think up. Maybe a shootin' contest, or puttin' a few blastin' caps here an' there to see what they'd do. I ain't never done in no deppity marshal before."

"Too bad, Duff," a second man said with a trace of sarcasm. "I know the boss musta hated to take all that fun away from you, but he's bound to have some good cause for wantin' him alive."

"Yeh, I s'pose."

The footsteps came toward Ridge and unseen hands took hold of him and turned him over so he faced the interior of the room. Behind the heavy leather boots and muddy trouser legs directly in front of Ridge's face, he saw chair and table legs in the center of the room, a squat iron stove along the far wall, and a wide, low cot to one side. One boot drew back and casually crashed into his upper chest.

"You hear that, mister deppity you-ass marshal? The boss won't let me skin your hide an' hang it out to dry . . . not yet, anyway. Don't you feel like one lucky son of a bitch? Huh, mister deppity you-ass marshal?" Turning his head back to his companion, Ridge's tormenter chuckled and said, "I don't believe he wants to discuss it right now, Hutch."

Hutch, over by the stove pouring himself a cup of coffee, laughed dutifully.

The boot drew back again and found a soft landing place in the middle of Ridge's belly, then Duff moved away and joined Hutch at the table.

"What'd Bramwell have to say 'bout them papers we sent him?" Duff asked, pouring a glass on the table half full of whiskey from a grimy, brown bottle.

"Seemed real pleased by it," Hutch said. "Said it might fit in with things real good an' that he knew jus' what to do with it."

"That's one smart hombre," Duff said with open admiration in his voice. "Figgerin' out this whole setup an' all. 'Fore this is over, he's gonna make us all stinkin' rich."

"Yeh, maybe," Hutch said. "But I don't like it, this marshal findin' his way here an' all, an' the way he killed Parnell an' Downs without us even knowin' it."

"We fixed that, didn't we? We got them extra guards out an' now won't nobody else get in shootin' distance of this canyon without us knowin' 'bout it. An' don't forget them little surprises we planted out there in the rocks. One little match can seal that south entrance tighter'n a gnat's ass."

"There'll be other marshals come after this one, an' maybe the army, too, purty soon."

"Yeh, but Bramwell will know 'bout it when it happens.. He wouldn't let us get trapped without some warnin'."

"Like he knew 'bout this marshal?" Hutch scoffed. "Hell, he told me they hired this Parkman feller here as a guard on one of the gold shipments. Thought he was jus' a drifter."

"You worry too much, Hutch," Duff growled. "Don't go yella on me now, boy. I won't stand for it."

"I ain't, Duff," Hutch said, his tone suddenly guarded. "I ain't goin' yella."

"That's 'nough of that yella talk, then," Duff said. "You leave the thinkin' to Bramwell an' the bossin' to me an' you'll be all right." He rose and strode to the door. Sticking his head out, he bellowed, "Woman! Food!" Then he returned to the table and sat down.

A moment later a drab, spiritless woman shuffled into the room and went to the stove to begin cooking.

That night and the following day were endless torture for Ridge Parkman. He was given neither food, water, nor any relief from the tangle of ropes which bound him. On the first evening he had received some continuing attention from the drunken Duff, who came over occasionally to taunt and abuse him, but eventually even that ended when the outlaw chief staggered over to collapse on the cot and drifted into loud, restless sleep.

The following morning the woman had brought a saucer of bacon grease over to rub on Ridge's raw and bleeding wrists and throat, but when she later brought a cup of water over and began to untie the gag around his mouth, she was scared off by footsteps outside before she could give Ridge a taste of the precious moisture. She did not risk coming near him again.

Toward evening of the second day, Duff and Hutch came to the cabin for another conference. Though by that time Ridge's mind was floating in a fog of near delirium, he forced his attention to focus on the talk of the two men.

Hutch swung a leg over the back of a chair and sat down at the table. "Big doin's in town," he announced, as Duff brought his bottle and glass over and sat down. "Man, that Max Bramwell is one slick operator.

He's done changed the whole deck on us in jus' one night."

"What's he up to?" Duff asked apprehensively. He was the sort of dull, plodding character who had a natural dislike for any sudden changes in his customary routine.

"Wal, we met for nearly half an hour out to the edge of town, an' he had the whole thing already figgered out for us. First, we're disbandin' this bunch. Bramwell says hold 'em here for four more days so's none of 'em can get into town an' mess up what he's got goin' there, then pay 'em off from the last raid an' tell 'em to get the hell outa this neck of the woods."

"No more gold?" Duff asked with dull alarm. "Is he cuttin' us out?"

"Naw, he's got plans for you an' me an' Thomas an' Sims. The rest he don't want round here to spoil things."

Hutch was talking quickly now, excited about the new plans of Bramwell which still seemed to have Duff anxious and bewildered. "You know that stuff in the marshal's papers 'bout ol' man Reynolds an' his troubles with the bank back in Philadelphia? Wal, Bramwell's let it leak out in town that Reynolds is a crooked banker from back east an' that he's come out here to cheat these folks here, too. He's got the miners believin' that Reynolds is the one leakin' the information about the gold shipments. Folks is gettin' plumb hot over there in De-Witt's Strike."

"So what's he doin' that for?" Duff asked. "I don't get it."

"Hell, Duff, think about it a minute. What would folks decide if they lynched ol' Reynolds an' then the gold robberies stopped all of a sudden? They'd think he was behind it all the time. Right? An' then here's this young girl who inherits a freight company that she don't know how to run an' don't know what to do with. An' her an orphan all by herself.

"Ol' Bramwell, he wants that woman an' he wants that freight company, an' jus' as soon as Reynolds stretches a rope, they're both his on a silver platter. Ain't that sweet?"

"So what 'bout us?" Duff asked. "What part of this new pie do we glom our teeth into?"

"We go in an' help Bramwell run the freight company. That's a kick, ain't it? Us guardin' the same gold shipments we used to steal."

Duff was nodding his head in slow under-standing, and eventually Bramwell's new plans began to appeal to him. "So all we got to do is jus' sit out here for a few days, pay the boys off, an' send 'em packin'. Right? An' then we move to town an' get respectable."

"That's 'bout the lot of it," Hutch said happily. "All, that is, 'cept the part about this feller over here." He pointed with his thumb at Ridge.

"What 'bout him?"

"Here's the way it goes," Hutch said. "This here Parkman, he's a real mean hombre. He's the one that Reynolds's been usin' to get word out about when to rob the gold shipments. But he ain't goin' to get away with it. Nosiree. He's gonna get hisself killed near town an' then hauled in as evidence of how crooked Reynolds is."

"I sure was hopin' I'd be the one that got to kill that there you-ass deppity," Duff said, glancing over at Ridge wistfully. "I ain't never done one before."

"Well, hell, Duff," Hutch said. "If it means that much to you, you could be the one. Jus' haul his carcass to the edge of town, blast him full of holes, an' carry him on in slung over a saddle. Bramwell said he'd do the rest. Got it all thought out, he does."

Duff leaned back in his chair and took a deep drink of the whiskey, a contented grin slowly spreading across his face. "That Bramwell," he said, "is one helluva smart hombre. He shore is."

Ridge had drifted away into unconsciousness. He had no idea how much time had passed or whether it was day or night when he felt hands roughly fumbling with the knots which had kept him immobile for so long. The pain this caused was tempered by the hope that he would now, at last, be freed for a while.

First his feet were untied, and then the ropes came off his neck and hands. "Get on your feet, deppity," Hutch's gruff voice commanded.

Ridge's first attempt to straighten his legs brought nothing but sharp stabs of pain which shot up from his twisted legs and raced straight up his backbone.

"Haul it up from there, mister," Hutch said. He reached down and pulled Ridge to his feet, but it was still a moment before Ridge could command the rebellious muscles in his legs to support him without help.

"Now jus' remember, deppity," Hutch warned. "The only reason we ain't shootin' you here is that the boss wants a fresh kill when we get out to town. But if you give us any trouble, I'll drop you now, anyway."

With his hands free at last, Ridge reached up and began working at the knotted bandanna, and Hutch allowed him to loosen it and remove the burlap from his mouth. His parched throat, scraped raw from the burlap fibers he had swallowed, was swollen nearly shut. As soon as he could force his legs to work, he headed for the water bucket which sat on a bench beside the stove. Again Hutch made no move to stop Ridge as he lifted the gourd dipper and took a few tentative swallows. It was difficult at first to force the water down his throat, but in a moment he had emptied the dipper and was reaching back in the bucket for more.

"Too bad for you that you had to go an' find us here," Hutch reflected. "I ain't a man for takin' too much pleasure in killin' — not like that crazy bastard Duff — but you done seen an' heard too much to stay alive now."

Ridge continued his drinking and would not have answered even if he could. But he thought, I ain't dead yet, buster, an' nothin' ain't certain 'til it happens. He could feel the strength and control returning to his cramped limbs, but he still feigned crippledness as he turned and staggered over to a chair to sit down.

In a few minutes a man Ridge had not seen before came to the cabin door and said, "Duff's ready, Hutch. Bring 'im out an' we'll get 'im tied to one of these horses."

"Let's go, deppity," Hutch said, drawing his pistol and pointing it at Ridge.

Outside, Duff and two other men were waiting, already mounted. With a flash of anger, Ridge saw that the big ugly Duff was sitting astride President Grant, and a quick glance at the horse showed that he was not getting the best of treatment from the outlaw chief. Long spur scratches down his flanks were crusted with dried blood.

Not only had Duff appropriated Ridge's horse, but he was also using Ridge's saddle and the marshal's two rifles, the Sharps .50 and the Winchester still hung where Ridge always kept them.

Ridge allowed himself to be hoisted onto one of the two extra horses. His hands were again tied together, and as an added precaution, Hutch tied the loose end of the rope to the saddle horn. He was allowed just enough slack to handle the reins.

They started out in single file toward the upper end of the canyon. Duff led the way with one other rider behind him. Ridge was kept in the center and Hutch and the fourth rider brought up the rear. The trail was a rugged one, a rough ride for both man and horse. It climbed sharply up out of the canyon, then descended rapidly down the opposite mountainside into a winding, rocky valley.

Ridge tried to look at the situation logically, searching for any possible means of escape, but he had to admit that it looked gloomy. If he just had his hands free, or if there was something less than four of them — but all the "ifs" did no good. He had to deal with things the way they were. He finally decided that his only remote hope was to wait for a reasonably open area and make a break for it. It would not work, of course, but at least he would go out trying.

For about the next half hour they followed a trail which rambled up and down the mountainsides, winding through tumbled masses of rock, wooded areas, and, in one place, around the perimeter of a sparkling blue mountain lake. When they cleared the lake, the trail straightened out for about fifty feet, then disappeared into a jumble of boulders and rocky outcroppings.

Ridge was the first to spot the figure up ahead as he stepped out from a hiding place in the rocks and kneeled. Instantly the man aimed his rifle and fired two quick shots no more than a second apart.

The man directly in front of Ridge went limp and tumbled sideways out of the saddle. On up ahead Duff was having trouble, too. He rode on for an instant like a rubber-limbed drunk, scarcely remaining on the horse as he fumbled ineffectively for his pistol. His shirt was ripped and stained crimson from the bullet exit wound in his lower back.

Finally the bandit chief was unseated as President Grant, spooked by the excitement and by the odd behavior on top of him, lurched forward and bolted down the trail. The second riderless horse leaped around Duff's falling body and ran after President Grant.

Ridge knew he had to act fast to avoid being shot by the two remaining outlaws behind him. He let go of his horse's reins, grabbed the saddle horn and fell sideways out of the saddle, letting his horse drag him roughly after the two running horses ahead.

By then shots were popping all around him. Up ahead the attacker, who Ridge had already realized was Oak, was levering out a deadly hail of bullets from his Winchester, but Hutch and the fourth outlaw were shooting now, too.

Ridge felt his horse stumble as the first shot hit him, and then start down as a second bullet smacked into the back of his head. Desperately he scrambled to get his feet under him and to stay clear as the dead horse fell. When the animal was down and still, Ridge curled up behind him and began working frantically at the knot which still kept him attached to the saddle horn.

A couple more shots thumped into the horse's carcass, and then suddenly the shooting stopped. Ridge froze and did not even risk raising his head up to see who had survived and who had died.

Oak leaped softly down from the rocks above Ridge to the ground beside him. Thin wisps of smoke still drifted lazily out of the barrel of the rifle he held in one hand. Wordlessly the Indian drew his knife and slashed the rope which bound Ridge to the saddle horn.

As Ridge held out his hands so Oak could cut them free, he said, "I shore wouldn't ever want to be on the other side from you in a scrap. It's downright unhealthy to be somebody you don't like."

"There was only four?" the Indian asked quietly. His voice was calm, and though he was still watchful, he seemed not the slightest bit excited by the battle he had just won.

"Jus' four," Ridge assured him. "I know they would of brought more if they knew they were goin' to run crossways of a wild Cherokee on the warpath."

"I would not desert a brother. We owe you

life for life. It is a bond between us. Now I will go for the soldiers."

"Wal, it's a good thing you didn't go yet, an' not jus' 'cause you saved my bacon from the wolves." He quickly told the Indian about the additional guards the outlaws had posted and the explosive charges which were planted to seal the south entrance to the valley. "You an' the army scouts are goin' to have to slip in an' take care of that business 'fore the troops can move in."

After a few moments of talk, Ridge sent Oak back down the trail to get him a revolver and gun belt while he himself went ahead to catch his horse. When he had walked on up the trail a couple of hundred feet he spotted President Grant and the other horse stopped and looking back nervously at him. Ridge whistled once and President Grant flicked his ears attentively, then came trotting back to him.

Ridge caught up the reins and patted the horse affectionately. "You're a welcome sight, ol' boy," he said. "I jus' wish I could bring ol' Duff back for a while so I could beat the hell outa him for rakin' them spurs into your hide."

In a moment Oak came trotting back up the trail and delivered a pistol and cartridge belt to Ridge. Ridge strapped the gun on, and then as he swung up onto the back of President Grant, he said, "I'm much obliged for the rescue, Oak, but we ain't got much time for handshakin' an' backslappin' now. You got 'bout three days to get them soldiers up here an' to get the job done, 'cause after that them polecats back there are goin' to scatter in 'leven different directions an' we'd never get 'em all hunted down.

"An' me," he added, turning the horse toward town, "I got a powerful hankerin' to do some shore 'nough tail kickin' over to DeWitt's Strike." With a click of his tongue and a slap of the reins against the horse's neck, he started quickly up the trail.

CHAPTER 13

Despite his eagerness to get on into town and to get his hands on Bramwell, preferably around the neck, Parkman made his approach to DeWitt's Strike cautiously. He did not know what kind of situation he would find there, but he did know that he had probably already been tagged as an outlaw, and since he was to have been killed on the edge of town, he thought Bramwell might have posted men along the trail to meet Duff and the others as they came in.

Long before he reached DeWitt's Strike, Ridge began making a wide circle which would lead him around to DeWitt's mine, hoping to find his friends there. He reached the mine about midafternoon, but found it empty. After searching inside the mine, he went down to the slag pile where they had kept their vigil on the freight office a few days before.

He could not tell what was going on below

in town, but by the size of the crowd which jammed the streets and from the noise which filtered up to him, he decided that something out of the ordinary was taking place. He watched for a moment longer, then mounted his horse and rode around so he could enter town from the north. It was not the direction from which he was expected and he thought he could probably get in unnoticed.

At the edge of town he tied his horse to a rail and started down to the other end of town where the excitement seemed to be centered. As he had expected, the crowd was the thickest and maddest and loudest near the DeWitt's Strike Freight Company office. Men were jammed shoulder to shoulder outside the building, shouting angrily, waving guns and clubs and ropes. The windows of the building were covered with heavy wooden shutters and rifle barrels protruded from several narrow slits around the walls.

Ridge, standing on the boardwalk of a saloon across the street, turned to a man beside him and said, "I jus' got here. What's all the commotion about?"

"That mangy skunk Reynolds that's been thievin' all our gold is holed up in there with some of his friends," the man said angrily.

"The town's done found him out fer what he is an' now we're goin' to put the rope to 'im."

"Who's in there?" Ridge asked.

"Reynolds an' that gal of his, an' a few of the guards that stuck by him. Ol' man De-Witt's in there, too. Musta been in cahoots all the time. An' some other ol' greasy rock cracker. Mr, Bramwell went in a while ago to try to talk 'em out. We'd of done burnt 'em out a long time ago if it wasn't for him."

"Bramwell's been tryin' to save 'em, huh? That's plumb noble of 'im."

"Yeh," the miner agreed. "He's the reason why we ain't hung that other feller already, too. The one we got over in the Last Nuggett. Some damn Dutchman name of Rieger, I think."

"A mighty reasonable man, that Bramwell," Ridge mumbled. "I guess he don't want to see nobody get hurt."

"He won't make it, though," the man growled. "There'll be corpses in this town 'fore the sun sets today."

"It looks like it." Ridge started to walk away, but just then the door of the freight company office opened to let Bramwell out, then closed quickly behind him.

Bramwell stopped on the porch of the office and held his hands up for the crowd to get quiet.

"Wal, are they comin' out?" somebody shouted from the crowd.

Bramwell looked around the crowd of angry men, his expression mixing just the right amount of worry and concern, and said, "They won't put themselves into the hands of a mob like this one, and I can't say that I blame them." He quickly quieted the uproar of protests by the crowd and then went on. "They said they would surrender, but only to U.S. marshals or the army."

"To hell with the marshals," somebody shouted. "Let's burn 'em out!" That idea was immediately popular with the crowd and shouts of "Burn 'em out!" rose everywhere.

Again Bramwell called for silence. "That's not smart, men," he shouted. "No matter what happens, we'll need this building to ship our gold out of here once this thing is over. There's no use burning it down when we'll need it later. An' don't forget about the gold that's already in there. How many of you are willin' to give that up just to get aholt of Reynolds?"

Parkman shook his head and grinned in reluctant admiration of the way Bramwell was handling the situation. In the end, of course, he would let the crowd have its way and hang Reynolds and the others, but he would come out of it looking like a reasonable man who had tried to do the right thing. He was probably counting on the crowd to go crazy when a dead body was hauled into town and denounced as Reynolds's messenger to the outlaws.

That thought made Ridge chuckle. No dead body would be hauled into town today, not unless somebody came across Duff and the three others and brought them in.

As Bramwell continued to talk and reason with the mob, Ridge started away down the street toward the Last Nuggett. The first thing he had to do was get Dolf out of the predicament he was in before some of these whiskey-primed, overanxious miners decided to take out a little of their wrath on him by looping a rope around his neck and leaving his feet dangling.

Two bartenders in the Last Nuggett were busy pouring liquid courage into shot glasses as quickly as they could move up and down the long plank bar. The tone in the place was ugly and the talk was mostly of burning and bullets and death. Ridge waded into the crowd as if he was trying to get to the bar, but he actually did not have any time for drinking. He was more concerned with trying to discover where Dolf was being held.

At the back of the saloon, in front of the rear door which led to the back rooms where the saloon girls took their customers for entertainment, two men were sitting with their rifles in hand. Ridge knew this saloon did not employ any sort of armed guards or bouncers, so he decided that the pair must be guarding the entrance to the back rooms instead. That had to be where Dolf was.

It would be suicide, though, to try and get past them. Even if he could take the two men by themselves, he would not stand a chance against the saloon full of angry men who would back the guards up. He turned and started back toward the front entrance.

Once outside, he slipped around the side of the building to the back. Things looked a little more promising there. Only one man holding a shotgun guarded the back entrance to the building.

Ridge thought for a moment, then finally started around the corner, staggering erratically and occasionally using the wall of the building to stop himself from swaying off balance and falling down. The guard turned the shotgun toward Ridge, but did not seem overly alarmed by the presence of a drunk.

Ridge staggered up to the guard and reached for the latch of the door, but the guard stopped him by holding the barrel of the shotgun in front of him. "You can't go in there, buster."

"I come to see ol' Kate," Ridge slurred. "She's awaitin' for me in there."

"Ain't none of the girls in there now," the guard said, "so git on outa here 'fore I wallop you one with this here scatter-gun."

"No girls?" Ridge said. "No girls. With, hell. . . ." He turned partially away as if he was about to stagger off, then spun back quickly, planting his right fist squarely on the man's jaw. Ridge caught him as he fell and dragged him out of sight around the corner of the shed behind the saloon. Then he retrieved the shotgun and cautiously opened the back door.

About midway down the long hall of the building sat another guard in front of a door. When that guard saw Ridge, he rose and pointed his rifle down the hall toward him. As Ridge stepped inside, he turned and said something over his shoulder as if he was speaking to the guard outside. Then he started down the hall toward the man.

"Bramwell told me to come over an' take over for you so you could go get a bite," Ridge told the guard.

The man looked at Ridge suspiciously for a moment, then lowered the muzzle of his rifle and said, "I wished I knew what the hell was goin' on round here. First they send me over here to guard this Dutchman, an' then they tell me to go eat. I didn't volunteer for this business, you know. I was all for jus' slingin' a rope over a tree limb an' bein' done with him, but that big-shot Bramwell started buttin' in an' tellin' everybody what to do."

"Things is fixin' to get even more confusin' for you, brother," Ridge said as he approached the man. Without warning he swung the butt of the shotgun up and popped the guard on the side of the head, knocking him neatly back into the chair behind him.

He propped the guard up in the chair and laid the rifle across his lap, putting one of his hands across the stock. It probably wouldn't fool anybody, Ridge thought, but somehow it seemed better than leaving the fellow sprawled out in the middle of the floor.

The door to the room was unlocked and there was no guard inside the tiny cubicle. About two thirds of the space in the room was taken up by a large double bed with an iron bedstead. Dolf was sitting on the floor at the foot of the bed, his arms stuck back through the rungs of the footboard and tied together. His mouth was gagged with a strip of white cloth ripped from a sheet.

Dolf's eyes widened in surprise as he saw Ridge enter the room. As Ridge stooped beside the miner and began working at the knotted rope, he said, "This is a mighty odd way to be found in a lady's bed an' business room, Dolf. Reckon what Miss Reynolds would think if she saw you trussed up in here amongst all this red sateen an' lilac smellum?"

He didn't give Dolf a chance to answer, but motioned for him to be quiet as he removed the gag from his mouth. "Keep it low, pard," he said. "We gotta hightail it 'fore somebody else comes back here to check on you."

The room had one window, but the alley it opened onto was visible from the street and Ridge decided they should not try to go out that way. He led Dolf back out into the hallway and then out the back door. Within a couple of minutes they were safely away, headed back toward the deserted end of town where Ridge had left his horse.

When they reached President Grant, Ridge drew his carbine from the boot and told Dolf, "You take my horse an' light outa here. Head up to DeWitt's mine an' wait there 'til we can get this thing cleared up. I'm goin' to try an' get into that freight office somehow."

"No," Dolf told him stubbornly. "I ain't goin'."

Ridge turned to the miner, glowering angrily as he said, "That wasn't no request, mister. It was an order. I'm goin' to have enough trouble on my hands without tryin' to protect you from the mob that'll be comin' after you as soon as they find those men I bashed."

"You need me," Dolf insisted. "I know a way to get back into that freight office without bein' caught."

"How's that?" Ridge asked.

"I was in there before. When the town started gettin' stirred up by the talk that was goin' around about Reynolds, me an' Abe an' Mike DeWitt went there to warn Reynolds an' his daughter, an' to help protect them if it came to that.

"Well, the crowd started gatherin' fast, an' pretty quick we knew we had some real trouble comin'. It was then we decided that one of us had to get out an' ride like hell down to Adobe City to try an' get some help 'fore everybody in there got lynched."

"Yeh, but that don't tell me how we're

180

goin' to get in there."

"There's a trapdoor an' a tunnel," Dolf said. "It comes up in the floor of that little stock shed behind the freight office. But like a bunch of dummies, we didn't think that Bramwell knew 'bout the tunnel an' that he'd post a guard on the back door of it. When I come crawlin' up outa that hole, the first thing I saw was a gun pointin' at my nose."

"Was there jus' one guard on the tunnel?" Ridge asked.

"There was when I come out of it."

"Okay, you stay an' go with me," Ridge decided. "There's no use in either of us headin' down to Adobe City now 'cause Oak is already halfway there by now, an' he'll be sendin' help. I jus' hope it'll come in time. It'll be at least a day an' a half 'fore anybody can cover that much ground."

He got his Sharps rifle from his saddle and gave it to Dolf to carry, along with two boxes of spare cartridges. Then the two of them headed in a roundabout route toward the rear of the freight office, avoiding as best they could the crowd of men who were mobbed around the building.

The shed was about fifty yards away from the rear of the freight company building and well clear of seventy-five or so men who were milling around watching the back door.

Ridge stepped up to the door of the shed and tapped on it lightly. "Who is it?" a voice called out from inside.

"Bramwell sent me to take over for you," Ridge said, deciding that the same ruse might work one more time.

"The hell he did," the voice inside said.

Ridge opened the door and was about to say something about getting some food. At the same time, he and the man inside recognized one another. It was the clerk who had worked in the front of the freight company office.

"You!" the guard said. He started to bring up his rifle for a shot, but he never made it. The bullet from Ridge's revolver caught him squarely in the belly and flung him back like a limp rag.

Ridge and Dolf leaped into the shed just as the first of the nearby men started shouting and rushing over. Ridge slammed a couple of shots wildly out the wall of the shed to postpone the rush of the mob as he flung open the trapdoor and leaped inside the tunnel. Dolf was close behind, making it in only a fraction of a second before a barrage of shots riddled the building.

CHAPTER 14

Ridge had fallen the full ten-foot depth of the shaft without even realizing there was a ladder there to use. Then Dolf came tumbling down on top of him, but neither of them was injured. Immediately Dolf began scrambling away on his hands and knees through a long, dark tunnel. Ridge followed.

Behind them gunfire continued to plaster the shed, and Ridge realized that none of the men at the rear of the building apparently knew it contained a tunnel entrance.

After one short bend, they were in total darkness and the noise of the shots grew faint. "It's not far," Dolf called back as he continued to crawl.

Then up ahead they heard a voice which Ridge immediately recognized as Abe's. "Jes' hold it in there, whoever you are," he warned. "I got 'nough dynamite planted down there to turn that hole into one long grave, an' I'm jes' a'itchin' to put a match to it."

"It's us, you ol' fool," Dolf called out angrily. "Don't blow it up. It's Dolf an' Ridge down here."

"Wal how in thunder am I s'posed to know, you ornery Dutchman?" Abe grumbled. "You ain't neither one of you s'posed to be here."

In a couple of minutes they reached the opposite end of the tunnel and climbed up into what was apparently the vault room of the building.

Abe slapped Ridge's back heartily and said, "You're a sight to behold, son. We'd plumb give up on you an' the Injun. Figgered you musta been kilt somewheres by them raiders."

"I mite near was," Ridge admitted, "but Oak, he saved my bacon for me. That's one mean fighter, that Cherokee."

"Yeh, he is. I wished we had him here right now to help us hold off that mob out there when they make their play."

"He's gone for soldiers," Ridge said. "We found the outlaw camp an' it'll be all over for them if the army can get there in time."

Turning to Dolf, Abe asked, "You didn't make it, huh, pardner?"

"They were watchin' the other end of the

tunnel," Dolf said, "an' they caught me right off. Ridge got me loose, though."

Dusting the dirt off his rifle and heading to the door of the room, Ridge said, "Wal, let's check this situation out an' see how bad it is."

"Plumb bad," Abe mumbled as he and Dolf followed him out.

The first room they came to was one which faced toward the rear of the building. Mike DeWitt and two other men were on guard there, sitting on the floor with their rifles pointed out the gun slots cut in the back wall. Ridge noticed with approval that they had piled sacks of grain and other boxes of supplies along the bottom portion of the wall so that the bullets from the mob outside would not penetrate through to them.

Without getting up, DeWitt turned his head to see who had come in. When he spotted Ridge, he shook his head and said, "Welcome to hell, marshal. We kin use you."

"It's some predicament," Ridge agreed, "but I think there's help on the way if we can jus' hold out for a while, maybe a day or so."

"It's a long time to keep that pack of wolves out there at bay," one of the other men said.

Suddenly several shots sounded outside and a handful of bullets slammed through the wall of the building. Ridge, Abe, and Dolf dropped to the floor behind the protective barricade around the bottom half of the wall.

"Don't shoot, men," Ridge told the three men by the wall. "I don't want no more killin' than absolutely has to be, an' there ain't no use wastin' ammunition unless they try to storm the place."

"We been holdin' off," DeWitt agreed. "Me an' the boys got friends out there, an' we ain't hankerin' to dispatch none of 'em 'less we have to."

As Ridge and Dolf turned and started toward the front of the building, Abe went back in the vault room. "I'd best get back to that tunnel," he said, "in case somebody gets a bright idee 'bout comin' in to take a look around."

"Okay," Ridge told him, "but don't blow it unless you absolutely have to. A shot or two will probably keep it clear, an' we may need it later if they put the torch to this place."

Parkman and Dolf went down a hallway which led to the large front room of the building. There they found Reynolds and his daughter, as well as two other guards

186

Ridge recognized immediately as Nimblett and Fawcett, his fellow survivors from the abortive gold run several days before.

This portion of the building had been barricaded similar to the back so that anyone who stayed down below waist height was safe from any shots which might come in from the outside.

Reynolds's face, drawn and somber by the ordeal, brightened some at the sight of Ridge and Dolf. "At last, a representative of the law," he said. "Now maybe you can put an end to this situation and get us out of this dangerous dilemma."

"I'm afraid it ain't goin' to be that easy," Ridge said. He told them about his capture by the outlaws and about Bramwell's plans to frame Ridge as the outlaw messenger for Reynolds. "If I set one foot out there an' try to tell 'em I'm the law, Bramwell'd have me killed 'fore I could blink an eye."

"What a mess," Reynolds said, shaking his head despondently. "I just can't believe everything that's happening lately — Max Bramwell turning on us so quickly, and all those men out there actually believing that I've engineered a scheme to kill my own guards and rob my own gold shipments. It's all so preposterous."

"I guess we've all played right into Bramwell's hands — even me," Ridge said. He explained to Reynolds about the message he had been carrying when he was captured and how Bramwell had learned from it about Reynolds's banking troubles in Philadelphia.

"So that's how he found out," Reynolds exclaimed. "I want you to know, marshal, all of you, that I am innocent of those charges. It's just that I had no way to prove my innocence and so I had to leave to avoid the possibility of going to jail and humiliating my daughter. Maybe, though," he added dejectedly, "it would have been better to stay there. The disgrace of having her father in prison would not have been as terrible as dying at the hands of a bunch of lunatic miners."

"Wal, I think your daughter's safe enough," Ridge said. "Bramwell's set his cap to marry her, an' he wouldn't let nobody harm his future bride."

"I'd die before I would marry him!" Marjorie Reynolds exclaimed hotly.

"Bramwell would die if he tried it," Dolf said in a low, bitter voice. Ridge noticed that Dolf had eased around and was now sitting beside Marjorie along the back wall. The girl glanced up at her self-proclaimed protector with an unmistakable look of admiration in her eyes. Ridge did not comment.

He moved to the front of the room and greeted Nimblett and Fawcett, shaking their hands and reassuring them that they had made the right choice in sticking by Reynolds.

"We didn't neither one of us ever trust that feller Bramwell," Fawcett told Ridge. "Even 'fore this business started, we'd talked 'bout how there was somethin' not quite square 'bout him."

"Yeh," Nimblett agreed. "Then when all the talk started round town, we knowed we'd better get over here 'cause Mr. Reynolds would be needin' some help."

Inspecting the preparations that had been made for the battle they seemed about to face, Ridge was satisfied that everything was done that could be done. Each of the guards had two extra rifles beside him and all the ammunition he would need for an extended siege. There was plenty of food, too, and a fifty-gallon barrel of water stored in a back room would ensure that they would not go thirsty for a while.

Assuming that Bramwell could keep the men in town from burning the building, Ridge decided that the nine men inside stood a pretty good chance of defending the place for quite some time. The men outside might be mad as hell, but he doubted that very many of them would be willing to throw their lives into the breach by mounting a full-scale charge on the building. These carbines they had inside could throw a lot of lead in a hurry if the need came, and the defenders would be reasonably safe from any shots fired from the outside.

Ridge had returned to Reynolds's side and the two of them were talking quietly when somebody outside fired a potshot at the building. The bullet smashed through one of the shutters, broke a pane of glass, and thunked harmlessly into the back wall of the room. Everybody was down low and safe from such sniping.

Fawcett pumped three quick shots out into the street and immediately the noise of the crowd rose as they began to scramble for cover. "Jus' wanted to give 'em somethin' to think about," Fawcett said.

"Okay, but don't drop nobody unless you have to," Ridge said. He cautioned all of them that the less bloodshed there was at this point, the easier it would be to get everything settled once help arrived.

But the warning shots had been enough to drive the mob back behind barricades and buildings, and for a while there was no more activity either outside or inside the building. Ridge sent Dolf to the back room to aid the three men there and he himself took up a position on the front wall. The false calm of the impasse continued as the sun slowly dropped down the western sky and passed out of sight behind the mountains.

Near dusk, Marjorie prepared a meal of canned meat, beans, and corn bread which she carried around and served to the men on guard. The atmosphere in the building grew more tense as full darkness approached. Luckily the moon would be up tonight and there would be some light outside for the guards to watch by, but Ridge feared that the partial cover of darkness might spark some courage in the men outside. And, too, he was sure that business in the saloons in town was undoubtedly still booming — whiskey and anger made an explosive combination.

CHAPTER 15

At sundown Ridge put the men on an alternating schedule of rest and guard duty. He knew that the night would be a long one and that all of them would need at least some rest if they were to be awake and alert to fight. They rested in shifts of two hours off and two hours on, curling up along the walls so they would be immediately in place if a fight began.

Feeling somewhat guilty, Ridge took one of the first rest periods himself. His body had not yet fully recovered from the ordeal of spending nearly two days tied up in the outlaw camp, and the ride into town and the rescue of Dolf had just about pushed him to the limit of his endurance.

Marjorie had brought some salve to treat the painful rope burns on his neck, wrists, and ankles, and then he had taken a couple of the blankets she had given out to the men and stretched out beneath his gun slot. He fell almost immediately into an exhausted sleep.

The rattle of gunfire at the rear of the building ended his rest, and the subsequent explosion brought him fully awake and to his feet. Snatching up his rifle, he issued hurried orders to Reynolds and the other men to stay up front, then rushed down the corridor to the back room.

The shooting had stopped by the time he got there.

Turning in the darkness toward the sound of Ridge's approaching footsteps, DeWitt said, "They tried to rush us. 'Bout fifteen or twenty of 'em, I reckon. We drove most of 'em back, but I guess one of the ones that kept comin' was carryin' some dynamite an' it stopped a round. 'Fore we knew what happened, there was this boom an' a man jus' plumb disappeared. Damnedest thing I ever seen."

"I don't reckon they'll try that again," another of the men said.

"Not none of the bright ones anyhow," DeWitt agreed.

"Everybody okay back here?" Parkman asked.

The room was so dark that it was impossible to see anyone or anything. DeWitt and the other two men responded that they were unhurt, but Dolf said nothing.

"Dolf?" Ridge asked. "You all right?"

Still there was no answer.

Ridge moved toward where Dolf had been, almost stumbling over the miner's body sprawled on the floor. He reached out and his hand touched a warm, sticky wetness. Anxiously Parkman fumbled in his pockets for a match and struck it on his boot.

Dolf lay back on the floor. His arms were splayed out to his sides and his head and face were covered with blood.

"Dear God, no!" Marjorie Reynolds exclaimed from behind Ridge. He had not noticed that the girl had followed him from the front, but now she knelt beside him and by the light of his match began examining the wound.

"Is the Dutchman dead?" Abe asked from the doorway of the room he guarded.

Marjorie, who had been swabbing away the blood with a corner of a blanket, said, "I don't think so. It hit him in the top of his head, up in the hair." As her fingers began to probe through Dolf's hair, the match flame reached Ridge's fingers. He blew it out and lit another.

Marjorie had pulled her skirt back and was now tearing off strips of petticoat with

194

quiet efficiency. "I'll take care of him," she told Ridge, "but I'll have to light a lamp for a while."

"Bring him in here," Abe suggested. "Ain't no outside walls an' there ain't no way a bullet could hit a lamp."

"Okay, you two handle it," Ridge said. "I'll get back up front in case they try the same thing up there."

He went back to the front room and told the others that Dolf had been hit but that it might not be too serious. He did not try to go back to sleep. The little rest he got had done him some good and he relieved Nimblett so he could get some rest.

The hours moved by slowly. Down the street in both directions the town had come alive in its usual evening revelry, but there was little activity or traffic in the vicinity of the freight office or the building directly opposite from it. Men with guns were still watching and waiting out there.

About midnight Ridge noticed some activity on the boardwalk of the building across the street. Men were moving around behind the crude barricades there and Ridge and Fawcett tensed themselves for action.

Then a voice called out across the street. "You, in there! — Reynolds." It was Bramwell's voice. "Herbert Reynolds."

Reynolds was asleep on the floor near Ridge. Ridge went over and shook him to wake him. "Bramwell's out there callin' to you," he said.

"Can you hear me, Reynolds?" Bramwell called out.

Reynolds moved to one of the gun openings and said, "I'm here, Bramwell. What do you want?"

"Send the girl out, Reynolds. I don't want to see her hurt an' I promise you she will be safe no matter what happens."

"He must be out of his mind," Reynolds mumbled to Ridge, "to think I would even consider putting my daughter in his hands."

Ridge thought about it for a moment and then said, "Now wait a minute, Mr. Reynolds. Let's chew on this thing awhile 'fore you decide for certain." He turned to one of the gun holes and said, "Hang on out there, Bramwell."

"How could I possibly send her out there to him?" Reynolds asked in amazement.

"I think he's playin' it straight with this one," Ridge reasoned. "He's made the offer in front of everybody an' I don't think they'd let him turn around and use her against us.

"Let's face it," Parkman went on. "This here predicament looks plumb grim for the lot of us. But if your daughter has the chance to get out of the middle of it, she should take it. Then if things work out okay, she'll be out there waitin', an' if not . . . well, she'd be alive at least."

Reynolds considered the logic for a moment and then said, "We'll talk to her about it."

They went back to the vault room where Marjorie was nursing the still-unconscious Dolf. She looked up at them as they entered and said, "We got the bleeding stopped and he's resting better. I think now he'll make it all right."

"Honey," Reynolds began, "Bramwell has offered to let you go out and he promised you would not be harmed. We don't know how long this siege will last or what's going to happen, and I think you should go."

The girl looked up at her father and Ridge, and the sudden anger on her face was revealed in the dim lamplight. "That's out of the question, Dad!" she exclaimed. "I refuse to leave, especially with Dolf injured and needing care."

"Ma'am, I think it'd be better all round if you'd —" Ridge began.

But the girl interrupted him. "You men! You think you've got the sole right in the world to be brave and to fight when it's necessary to fight. But you don't! If you throw me out of here, I'll be fighting and screaming all the way, and the first thing I'll do once I get outside will be to get a gun and try to shoot Max Bramwell!"

Ridge listened to the girl's protests and then turned to her father. "Looks like she don't exactly agree with us," he said with a note of admiration in his voice. "I reckon if she feels that strong about it, she's got the right to get shot down or burnt up right along with the rest of us."

"Her mind is apparently made up," Reynolds agreed.

When they returned to the front of the building, instead of communicating the girl's refusal, Ridge called out, "Bramwell, this is Ridge Parkman."

"I knew you were in there, Parkman," Bramwell answered. "An' I won't be forgettin' that you killed a friend of mine gettin' inside there."

"Bramwell, I'm a United States deputy marshal an' as of this moment I'm placin' you under arrest for murder, attempted murder, an' robbery. An' by the time I get outa here, I'll have another dozen charges to pin on your worthless hide."

The laughter of the men behind the barricades showed that Bramwell had already spread his version of who Parkman was and why he was in DeWitt's Strike.

"I'm shakin' in my boots, mister marshal sir," Bramwell taunted. "Hell, every man out here's gettin' ready to throw up his hands an' surrender right now." The laughter rose again.

"I don't want 'em all," Ridge called out "Jus' you an' a few of the others that's been helpin' you steal that gold."

"I'm gettin' tired of your jokes, Parkman. They aren't funny, an' the men out here have a different idea about who'll be stretchin' ropes for murder an' robbery. Now what about the girl?"

"My daughter is not coming out," Reynolds said.

"It's her funeral, old man. At least I tried."

There were erratic exchanges of gunfire all through the night, but none of the men in town got drunk enough again or foolish enough to try another charge on the shipping company office.

As the night wore on, Ridge became more and more worried about the possibility of fire. Bramwell, of course, had no way of knowing that Oak had been sent for help, so he could not be immediately worried about the arrival of any lawmen or soldiers from Adobe City. But he must realize that someone with authority would hear about the situation eventually and come to investigate it. Bramwell would want the whole thing to be over when that happened. Then only his side of the story would be left to be told.

Parkman had taken one more rest period during the night, but was back on guard when the welcome sight of dawn began to appear along the fringes of the mountains to the east. Much of the town had finally gone to sleep a few hours before, but the freight office was still ringed by sleepy miners and townsmen who kept up the vigil.

The first bright shafts of the rising sun had just begun streaking across the town when the man came into view, riding his tired horse up the trail from the direction of Adobe City.

At first nobody paid much attention to him, but when he neared the freight office, men on both sides began to watch him closely. At last somebody behind one of the barricades called out to him. "You'd best stay on down yonder there, mister. It ain't healthy to go no further."

The rider sat straight in the saddle, a tall man with a lean muscular body and an unyielding face. His cold, direct gaze from beneath the pulled-down brim of his brown hat seemed to take in everybody and everything around him in a glance. His left hand was resting on the saddle horn, lightly holding his horse's reins, and his right hand was straight down his side close to the butt of his sidearm. As he rode slowly out from the shadows into the sunlight, the star pinned above the breast pocket of his shirt shone out brightly.

With one finger he reached up and pushed his hat back further on his head as he looked toward the man who had issued the warning to him. "I'm Marshal Zack Pitts from Adobe City an' I'm lookin' for Ridge Parkman," he said in a deep voice laden with authority.

"He's right over yonder in the freight office," one of the men behind the barricade said. "He's all yours if you can get 'im out of there."

Pitts turned his head and surveyed the freight office a moment, noting the pockmarks of bullet holes which scarred its walls. "You in there, Parkman?" he called out.

"Shore am, Pitts," Ridge answered. The two men had never met, but each knew the other by the reputations they had earned in the business. Parkman knew Pitts was one of the toughest and most competent men in

Henry Lott's Adobe City crew. "Reckon I can't exactly come out an' welcome you to town at the moment, though," Ridge went on. "We got ourselves a sort of Mexican standoff goin' right now."

"Okay," Pitts said unemotionally. He stepped to the ground and added, "We'll fix that." He looped his horse's reins over the rail in front of the freight office, then turned and faced across the street toward the barricades. "You men git," he told the several besiegers who were now watching him spellbound, scarcely able to believe how quickly he had come in and taken over. "In five minutes, every man I see holding a gun is goin' to be under arrest for interfering with a lawman."

The pronouncement threw the group into confusion, but none of them immediately complied with the order. Pitts stood his ground, silently watching and waiting, both hands hanging freely at his sides, ready to reach for the twin revolvers he wore in crossed gun belts.

Then Bramwell came striding down the street, flanked by half a dozen hard cases. As soon as Pitts had identified himself, someone had thought to go after Bramwell in the saloon where he had gone for a meal and a drink.

Ridge did not like the looks of the men who came along behind Bramwell, and he suspected that these were not just ordinary miners or gold country drifters. They were probably gunhands on his payroll.

Bramwell stopped on the boardwalk near the barricades and asked sternly, "What's goin' on here? Who are you, mister?"

Pitts did not answer, but merely stood for a moment staring at Bramwell, studying his features. When he at last seemed satisfied, he said simply, "Jack Kirk, you're under arrest."

Ridge realized then that Zack Pitts was the man Henry Lott had sent to identify Max Bramwell as the outlaw Jack Kirk of the California goldfields. That accounted for Pitts's early arrival. He must have been on his way to DeWitt's Strike even before Oak reached Adobe City with the news Ridge had sent.

From the boardwalk behind the newly arrived marshal, Ridge spoke up. "I'll make a deal with you, Pitts," he said. "You can have him as Jack Kirk when I get done with him as Max Bramwell — if there's anything left when I get done."

When Ridge saw Bramwell and his men coming, he had sensed trouble for Pitts and had moved quickly to the door to go out and back up his fellow marshal. He was not going to let Pitts ride into the middle of a snake pit like this one and then have to stand alone to face so many guns. He moved up and stopped beside Pitts.

A few minutes earlier that would have been a suicidal move for Parkman, but Pitts's arrival and the air of authority with which he had seized control of the situation had caused the townspeople, moments before thirsty for blood, to now back off and wait to see what was really going on. None seemed particularly eager to back Bramwell up anymore.

Bramwell quickly saw that and did not even try to carry his lies any further. For a moment it was a battle of nerves, with two lawmen facing seven desperadoes, and a horde of bystanders slowly backing away from where the action would soon begin — but not too far away. None of them wanted to miss seeing a thing.

When the shooting started, guns appeared in hands so quickly that in later retellings of the event, hardly anybody would agree on who had drawn first.

Ridge Parkman dropped to a crouch as he cut loose with his first couple of shots, then tumbled sideways and rolled once, coming up on his elbows with his gun still roaring.

Alongside Parkman, Pitts had made a similar movement, but in the opposite direction. Behind them, the rifles of Nimblett and Fawcett had kept up a steady racket for the several seconds that it took for the gunfight to run its bloody course.

Then suddenly there was silence. A morning breeze bumped against the thick cloud of gunsmoke in the street, stirred it tentatively, and began pushing it slowly away.

Ridge waited a moment, then rose carefully up onto one knee. A quick glance sideways told him that Pitts was still alive, kneeling about ten feet away. His right arm hung limply at his side, but his left hand still held a smoking pistol pointed toward where Bramwell and his men had been standing a moment before.

None of them were standing now. Five riddled bodies lay sprawled across the barricades, boardwalk, and in the street. A sixth man sat with his back against the wall of a building, his glazed eyes staring down in bewilderment at the hole in his belly. His head raised up until he was looking at the two lawmen in the street, and slowly his right hand began to lift the pistol it held. Pitts saw the move and calmly finished the outlaw with a quick shot.

Ridge rose slowly to his feet and began to

look around at the gathered spectators, trying to determine if any of them were going to cause any trouble. Behind him the defenders of the freight office had moved out onto the boardwalk in front of the building, their rifles pointed menacingly. It was a pleasure for them to be the aggressors at last.

"Anybody here want some of the same?" Parkman asked. Nobody answered. Beside him Pitts tried to stand up, but could not make it. The flow of blood from a second wound in his leg was staining his trousers crimson.

As Nimblett and Fawcett came forward to assist the downed marshal, Ridge went over to the dead men and began to look them over. Bramwell was not among them.

His mind flashed back to the instant before the gunfight began. Bramwell had been standing near one of the barricades when the shooting started up. Instead of fighting, he must have leaped down out of sight, leaving his men to die without him, and escaped in the smoke and confusion.

"Bramwell's hightailed it," Ridge called back over his shoulder as he turned and started running down the nearest alley.

He paused at the first corner and rounded it cautiously, gun drawn, but there was nobody in sight in either direction. His first impulse was to pick a direction and take off running, trusting his luck to go the right way and come across Bramwell. But after a moment's thought, he decided that it would be better to get help in the search.

Back in the street in front of the freight office, the two men were helping Zack Pitts into the building. The crowd of onlookers, which had numbered no more than twenty-five or thirty at the moment of the shoot-out, was quickly growing as the town awoke and moved in the direction of the freight office to find out what had happened.

Ridge stepped up onto the sidewalk and shouted for attention. "All right, everybody. Listen up." The crowd quieted and turned their attention to him. Suddenly, as a result of the action of the last few minutes, his authority was firmly established in the minds of the men gathered there.

"I want Bramwell an' I want him bad," Ridge said. "I want this whole town lookin' for that man, an' when he's found I want him brought here to me — alive. Now get goin'." The crowd quickly began to scatter, again glad to have a mission on the side of right.

Ridge stopped a group of several men who were moving down the street in front of him and said, "You men gather these bodies up an' get 'em down to the carpenter's shop for buryin'. If anybody can identify any of 'em, write their names down an' give 'em to me."

With that, he crossed the street and entered the freight company office. He wanted to make a quick check on Pitts and Dolf before he continued to organize the town to search for Bramwell.

CHAPTER 16

As a temporary headquarters in DeWitt's Strike, Henry Lott had chosen one of the tents that the cavalry had pitched on the edge of town near Gomez's corrals. The tent had been pitched for the use of the young lieutenant who led a squad of twelve horse soldiers to town with Lott, but the lieutenant had readily agreed to turn it over to the head marshal for his use.

Lott and the soldiers had arrived the day before, three days after the shoot-out with Bramwell and his henchmen. Lott had gone along with the cavalry troop on the raid on the outlaw camp in the mountains, and then, not knowing what sort of situation he would find in DeWitt's Strike, had requested that a few of the soldiers go on to town with him.

Ridge Parkman and Henry Lott were sitting at a table which had been commandeered from one of the nearby saloons, discussing the recent events and enjoying a bottle of bonded whiskey which Herbert Reynolds had given them. Zack Pitts was there, too, lying back on a cot and quietly sipping from a glass of the whiskey which Ridge had poured for him.

The wounds in Pitts's arm and leg had taken a lot out of him and his features were pale and drawn, but he had stubbornly refused to remain in the hotel room where he had been taken to rest and recuperate.

"I tell you, boys," Lott was telling the other two men, "it was one of the best operations of this size I've seen in twenty-seven years of bein' a lawman.

"A few miles out from the camp, we commenced to pickin' up stragglers, them that was the smartest an' knew the time was right to get out. We had four prisoners 'fore we ever got near where the main camp was. We stopped for the night 'bout two miles outside the camp 'cause that Indian, Oak, had warned us 'bout what was up ahead waitin' for us.

" 'Bout two hours before dawn, Oak an' the three army scouts went out to clear the guards out of the way, an' Captain Halliburton sent 'bout half his men on a roundabout route to block the north end.

"Then at dawn we started in, chargin' in

bold as brass from, both directions at once. They fought for a while an' kept us back, but when the Indian put the torch to a couple of their cabins, the fight went out of 'em an' they started givin' up. All in all, we sent twenty-two back alive an' dead, includin' the four we caught on the way up there."

"With the four Oak killed on the trail an' the six me an' Pitts dispatched here in town," Ridge figured, "that should be 'bout the lot of 'em. Couldn't have been too many of 'em got away . . . 'cept Bramwell."

"Yeah, Ridge," Lott said. "How in the devil could you let that happen, anyway?" Despite the question, there was little reproach in his tone. He seemed more aggravated at the unfortunate turn of events than he did about any possible carelessness by Parkman.

"It jus' happened, Henry," Ridge said. "For the life of me, I can't see how he could have done it, though. We watched the roads an' he couldn't have got out of town without somebody spottin' him, an' yet we did everythin' but tear the buildings down searchin' in town for him."

"He prob'ly had an escape plan worked out from the first day he got here," Pitts suggested from over on the cot. "That's the way he done out there in California. When

211

the fire got too hot, he jus' disappeared into the woodwork an' left his men to face the music. Things didn't go as smooth out there, though. The miners got to the gang members first, an' by the time the law arrived, there wasn't enough left of 'em to scoop up an' bury. Can't say I blamed the miners, though."

"Wal, what about the gold, Henry?" Ridge asked. "Was there any sign of it out to the outlaw camp when you took over?"

"All we recovered was what the men were paid off in," Lott said. "That was jus' a small part of what's been taken off all those gold shipments. Some of the prisoners we questioned said Bramwell had kept the biggest amount, but he didn't keep it at their camp. He never even went up there, but just sent orders along to them, an' then had Duff an' Hutch deliver the stolen gold back to him."

"So the gold's jus' as gone as Bramwell is," Ridge said.

"That's the way it shapes up right now, Ridge."

"Wal that's plenty bad, but I guess it ain't as bad as it would have been if Bramwell had done what he had in mind when we was holed up in that freight office. Zack, you shore was a welcome sight when you come ridin' down the middle of the street like Wyatt Earp hisself."

"Yeh, you were lucky Henry already had me started up here even before that Indian got there with word you'd found the outlaw camp."

"Well, enough of this backslappin', boys. We still got us some work to do 'fore we head the hoss toward home," Lott said. "Ridge, I'm callin' a town meetin' for tomorrow night, an' I want you to put the word out that I want every man to be there that's got two good legs an' ain't too drunk to crawl. Six o'clock, right out there in front of this tent.

"Right now you an' me have to go see this Reynolds feller an' get some things worked out with him. I've got word from back east about that trouble he was in, an' they've been tryin' to look him up for quite a spell now."

Leaving the bottle within reach of the invalid Pitts, Lott and Parkman left the tent and started down toward town.

They found Herbert Reynolds in his office, busy trying to reorganize his company and staff. He had, of course, kept the four guards who stayed by him, but several others had been fired and he was anxious to get a new, reliable guard force built up as quickly as possible. There was still gold in the DeWitt's Strike Freight Company office, and it still had to be protected on its way down to the vaults of Adobe City.

Reynolds welcomed the two marshals warmly and showed them to seats in his office before closing the door to the outer room.

"Marshal Lott," Reynolds said enthusiastically, "I don't have any adequate way to tell you how grateful I am for all the things you and the army have done. If it was not for all of you, especially Deputy Marshal Parkman here, I don't know . . . well, things would have no doubt had a much more tragic outcome by this time."

"It's our job," Lott said, shrugging off the thanks. "I'm just sorry we couldn't get around to cleanin' out that hornet's nest long before we did."

"Yes, that's true," Reynolds agreed. "The lives that were lost . . . but that's all history now. What can I do for you, sir?"

"Well, Reynolds, I hate to spring this on you so sudden-like, but I'm afraid you've got a long trip ahead of you. Back to Philadelphia."

Reynolds's smile faded and was replaced by an expression of concern. "I've been waiting for this," he said with gloomy acceptance. "I guess I was foolish to think I could run far enough to get beyond their reach. Still, though, it does seem a shame. I mean, after all the work I put into this business and all the turmoil we've been through, now that things are just beginning to show some promise, I must leave for a term in jail. But fate must be served, I suppose."

"No, Reynolds, I think you've got things a little confused here," Lott said. "There's a subpoena comin' for you, not an arrest warrant. From what I can tell of the facts they've sent me, the government's been sortin' through that mess ever since you've been gone, an' now they think they're about to get at the truth of it. They need you to help with the investigation and to be a witness against the real culprits. You won't be a defendant in the case."

Reynolds's face showed blank amazement as Lott's words began to soak in. "Well I'll be. . . ." he muttered quietly. "I'll be! You know, gentlemen, I'm fifty-two years old, and at my age, I finally decided that I had this world figured out for the wicked, unjust place that it is. But now all my cynicism has been shaken to its roots. Perhaps there is such a thing as justice after all."

"I've always thought there was, Mr. Reynolds," Ridge said quietly. "It's jus' that

215

sometimes it slips around on you an' comes in the back door."

Lott, not a particularly philosophical sort of man, was impatient to get the talk back to the matters at hand. "There still might be some problems in this for you, though," he told Reynolds. "They're in a big hurry for you to get back there. It'll mean you'll have to leave soon, maybe in the next day or two. I don't know what that'll do to your business here, but it's the way things gotta be."

"I'll figure something out," Reynolds said happily.

"My freedom and reputation are infinitely more valuable to me than this company."

Without a knock, the office door opened. The three men in the room looked up and saw Reynolds's daughter, Marjorie, enter, followed closely by Adolph Rieger, his head wrapped with a fresh white bandage. Marjorie had been a devoted nurse to the wounded miner, staying constantly by his side during the first crucial night while he was unconscious, and later pampering and protecting him like a fragile, wounded bird. Dolf had eagerly soaked up the attention. This was the first day she had permitted him up out of bed and out into the public for a meal and a stroll around town.

The girl's face lit up into a pretty smile when she saw Ridge and Lott in her father's office. "Our gallant defenders," she said. "How nice to see you, gentlemen." Both Ridge and Lott rose as she came in, then sat back down as she went around to kiss her father. "I have some news, Dad," she said.

"So do I, honey," Reynolds told her happily. "I have wonderful news." He eagerly told her about the turn of events back in Philadelphia and about the call for him to return. "It looks like we'll be going home soon, Daughter, at least for a while." He did not immediately notice his daughter's lack of enthusiasm about the trip.

"That's marvelous, Dad," she said hesitantly. "But I can't go back with you . . . I mean . . . I could, but I don't want to."

Reynolds looked at her in total confusion. "I can't leave you here, not a single young woman by herself. Even though this outlaw business seems to be cleared up, don't forget that this is still a very rough little town. And anyway, I thought you hated it out here and would be overjoyed to go back home for a while."

"Things are different now," she said. "That's what I wanted to tell you. You don't want to leave a single daughter here, but how do you feel about leaving a married one?" Her eyes went quickly over to Dolf, who was standing by the door as nervous as a schoolboy caught with a snake in class.

"My heavens!" Reynolds exclaimed. "Will you people *please* quit springing all these surprises on me? I'm just too old for so many at once." But his tone was light and it was obvious that the engagement pleased him.

Ridge was glad when Henry Lott rose to leave, saying, "You people have a lot to talk over, so I think me an' Ridge will get out of the way an' let you get to it. The soldiers an' I will be pulling out the day after tomorrow, Reynolds, an' I'd be obliged if you an' the gold was ready to leave then."

"Both of us will be quite ready," Reynolds promised him.

CHAPTER 17

The soldiers had spent part of the day building a small speaker's platform about eight feet square and four feet high in a large open area directly south of town. There was a festive spirit in the air as the people of DeWitt's Strike began gathering in its vicinity a good hour before the time set by Henry Lott for the town meeting to begin. By six that evening several hundred men and a few dozen women stood or sat in a large ring around the platform.

As with practically any other noteworthy event, good or bad, in the brief history of DeWitt's Strike, the gathering for the first town meeting was enriched with an ample supply of liquor.

Promptly at six Lott left his small tent office and elbowed his way through the crowd, flanked on one side by Ridge Parkman and on the other by Joshua Tinker, the lieutenant in charge of the troops in town. The chief marshal was not in a particularly good mood. He had not yet forgiven the people of the town for blundering so badly by following the perverse leadership of Max Bramwell, and was in no mood to deal very leniently with a town that had come so close to lynching one of the best deputy marshals in the state, and had stood by watching while another was shot down.

He climbed up on the platform and held up his hands for silence. The crowd lapsed into a semblance of quiet and order.

"The days of DeWitt's Strike as a wide-open, lawless little hellhole are over," he pronounced in a loud voice which reached every ear in the audience clearly. "The law's come to this place, an' it's here to stay, one way or the other."

A chorus of cheers went up at that pronouncement. Arms and bottles waved enthusiastically until Lott held up his hands for quiet again.

"Now you people can do it an easy way or a hard way. It's up to you to decide. If you care anything about this place, about your own lives an' property an' friends, you can set up your own local government with leaders, lawmen, laws, an' all the rest. That's the easy way.

"But if you hadn't got the guts an' grit to

do it for yourselves, I'm a sworn lawman an' I'll have to come in here an' do it for you. If it comes to that, God help you all! I'll come back with troops an' I'll impose martial law over the whole mining district. I'll close the doors of every saloon tighter'n a drum at eight every night, I'll ban gambling an' whores an' guns in town, an' I'll slap a dusk-to-dawn curfew on you. That'll be my kind of law, an' I'll make it stick!"

As Lott spoke, he paced the platform, emphasizing his speech by repeatedly slapping one fist into the palm of the other hand. Few, if any, in the crowd doubted the sincerity of his vows. Finally he paused for a moment, staring angrily out over the crowd almost as if daring anyone to catcall or challenge his word.

"Here's what I plan to do right now," Lott went on. "Before I leave here tomorrow, I'm goin' to appoint a temporary town leader and some temporary town marshals to keep order around here. As far as you're concerned, they'll have the authority of the United States marshals behind what they say an' what they tell you to do. If I hear they're not being obeyed, I'll be back up here 'fore you can spit in your whiskers.

"But the people I appoint are only goin' to be temporary in their jobs. One of the first things I've told the new town leader to do is organize a town election so you people can pick for your own selves who you want to hold the jobs.

"You people here, you miners an' businessmen an' everybody else, you been so busy grabbin' after gold that you wouldn't even take the time to organize yourselves an' make this place halfway fit to live in. Well, you've paid dearly for your greed. Now I've got a start made for you, an' the rest is up to you."

The applause which came from the crowd was markedly lacking in enthusiasm now, but Lott did not seem to notice. He waited for it to finish, then motioned for some nearby men to come up on the platform with him.

"I've appointed two men here," he went on, "as your first town marshals. Their names are Hugh Nimblett and Giles Fawcett, an' they'll pick as many men to help them as it takes to keep the law here. My man Ridge Parkman says they're good men, brave an' fair, an' you better back 'em up."

The two newly appointed lawmen had enough friends in the crowd that their names were fairly well received. They stepped forward and stood around grinning and feeling embarrassed for a moment as they were cheered, then stepped back.

"For town leader or mayor or whatever you want to call him," Lott went on, "I've picked the first man to find colors in this valley, Mike DeWitt."

The reception to his appointment was quite different. "That ol' drunk?" somebody shouted out, and the crowd began to laugh and jeer. DeWitt, who was standing on the platform near Lott, looked around the crowd apprehensively, but Lott merely waited out the uproar.

When the people had finally quieted, he said, " 'Fore any of you loudmouths start gettin' on your high horse an' thinkin' you could do a better job, jus' remember one thing. He was one of the few men in this town with sense enough not to believe Max Bramwell's lies an' run off half-cocked tryin' to burn buildings down on women an' hang United States marshals. He's mine an' Parkman's choice, an' if I find out he's gettin' drunk an' ain't doin' his job, I promise you I personally will come back up here an' kick his tail from hell to Thursday. That's all I got to say, I guess."

Abruptly Lott jumped to the ground in front of the platform and started off through the crowd toward his tent. Parkman and Lieutenant Tinker followed after him, and as they were leaving, Ridge heard DeWitt begin to take over the meeting.

CHAPTER 18

Behind the DeWitt's Strike Freight Company, drivers were buckling the last of their horses into harness as the guards began carrying the heavy wooden crates of gold out of the building to the wagons. Herbert Reynolds was supervising the operation in a fit of nervous frenzy.

The freight company owner had worked around the clock for the past two days hiring guards and drivers and trying to acquaint his daughter and Dolf Rieger with enough of the business that they could hold things down until he returned from Philadelphia. The young couple were planning to accompany Reynolds as far as Adobe City so they could first find a minister and get married, and then see Reynolds off on the train eastward.

Dolf and his two friends Abe and Oak had not exactly dissolved their mining partnership, but they had agreed that he should stay in town and help with the freight company until Reynolds got back. Then if he returned to the mine later, his share would be there waiting for him. Old Abe, however, had confided to Ridge that he doubted that Dolf would ever want to return to the Pipe Dream, and Ridge had agreed.

Ridge had spent the first of the early morning hours saying his good-byes to the few friends he had made in town. He ate breakfast with Abe and Oak in one of the town's best restaurants, defying anybody in the place to make even the slightest mention of the Indian's presence there. Then he dropped by the corrals to wish Gomez luck with his amorous pursuit of Maria.

Later he had gone by the newly established city police office to drink a cup of coffee and chat with Nimblett and Fawcett.

The only friend he had not yet been able to locate was Mayor Mike DeWitt. DeWitt had set up a city hall of sorts on the second floor above the carpenter's shop, sharing an office, desk, chair, and spittoon with a fast-talking land attorney, but he had not yet moved his personal belongings down to a hotel room and was still sleeping in his mine on the hill above town.

After checking every other likely place he

could think of, Ridge decided that DeWitt must still be up at the mine. He dropped by the army bivouac area where the soldiers were just taking down the tents and equipment. There he found Henry Lott and Lieutenant Tinker supervising the preparation of a wagon for Zack Pitts. Pitts sat on a chair nearby protesting heatedly that he could still straddle a horse with the best man in the outfit.

"Henry," Ridge said, reining President Grant up near the men. "I'm ridin' up to Mike DeWitt's mine to say so long to him. It won't take me long."

"Okay, Ridge. I'm surprised he's not down here to see us off. We'll be hittin' the trail in ten or fifteen minutes now."

"He must be down in the shaft somewhere lookin' for that danged disappearin' vein of gold. Maybe he don't know what time it is. Anyway, if I ain't back when you leave, I'll catch you on down the trail someplace."

When Ridge reached the mine, he was mildly surprised to find a saddled horse and two pack mules there, but he assumed that some prospector or miner friend must be there, perhaps spending the night in DeWitt's mine to avoid paying the high cost of a cot in town.

Parkman pushed back the board at the

entrance and stepped into the dark interior. He thought he could see the faint glow of a lamp or fire far back into the tunnel and called out, "Hey, Mike. Wasn't you goin' to come down for the sendoff this mornin'?"

There was no answer from the depths of the mine. DeWitt, Ridge assumed, must either be out of earshot or still asleep. He started carefully forward, moving toward the light ahead. In the area that DeWitt and the others had used for sleeping and eating during the watch on the freight office, a lit tin lamp sat in the middle of the passageway. DeWitt was lying on his blankets off to one side, his back toward the interior of the chamber.

"Roll outa them blankets, mayor," Ridge called out good-naturedly. "You can't get to be no big important politician if you sleep for half the day."

When DeWitt did not answer, Ridge moved forward, first touching the man's shoulder and then rolling him over onto his back. The side of the miner's head and cheek were blue-black and caked with sticky, drying blood, and the whole side of his head was swollen and puffy from the blow someone had planted there. Ridge checked him over quickly, leaning his head down and detecting a steady heartbeat.

He glanced around the tunnel for something with which to revive his friend. A wooden bucket was lying on the floor a few feet away, turned on its side and empty, but there was a canteen there, too, and Ridge got up to check and see if it contained any water.

Then Ridge heard the noise in the darker recesses of the mine shaft. It was a faint and seemingly far away rattle of rocks and gravel falling to the floor of the tunnel. He glanced at the lamp nervously, realizing how vulnerable its light made him to the attack of anybody hiding back there in the darkness. He quickly got the lamp and turned its wick down to the barest flicker, then set it in a niche in the wall where it barely illuminated the inside of the chamber.

Ridge stepped into the shadowy darkness along one wall and said, "Might as well come on outa there, whoever you are. There ain't no way out an' I'll be glad to wait here for as long as it takes to starve you out."

But, though he had said it, Ridge could not be absolutely certain that there was no other way out of the mine. Many times the miners dug air shafts straight up from the roofs of their mines to let stale air and gases out and to draw fresh air in. There could very possibly be one back there which was large enough for a man to crawl up through and escape.

It was no surprise to Ridge that nobody answered him and nobody came out and surrendered. He waited, gun drawn, for any sight or sound which might give him another clue to what was going on in here.

As the minutes passed, it occurred to him that maybe nobody was back there at all. The noise of falling debris was not uncommon in a mine, even when nobody was around to make it fall. Maybe somebody, an enemy or a thief, had come in and knocked DeWitt out and left again before Ridge arrived. But what about the horses and mules outside? They were certainly not DeWitt's.

Cautiously Ridge reached out and ran his hand along the wall, then took a careful, silent step forward. He was apprehensive about going on back into the depths of the mine, and not only because somebody might be lurking back there. DeWitt himself had pronounced this mine unsafe, and there was no telling what sort of catastrophes a man stumbling around in the darkness might bumble into. A weak timber might be nudged and displaced, causing a cave-in, or he might trip and fall into a hole that was dug in the floor to follow the capricious direction of a vein of gold.

But he had to at least try to check the situation out. It angered Ridge that somebody had so savagely attacked one of the men who was appointed only the day before to bring law and order to this area, and he was determined that whoever it was must be caught and made to account for what he had done.

As he continued to move on deeper into the mine, it seemed to Ridge that it took forever to make each step, placing his feet down lightly and carefully on the loose gravel and trying to make an absolute minimum of noise. He realized that in this darkness he could pass right by a still person only an arm's length away and never detect his presence, but he was trusting to the probability that whoever was in there would keep moving away from him rather than stay in one place and risk being found.

In what he judged to be at least half an hour, Ridge had only taken about a hundred steps. He wished now, belatedly, that he had taken a little time to familiarize himself with this part of the mine so that he would have some idea what direction the tunnel took and what lay ahead. Whoever was back there might know something about this mine, and that would be a tremendous advantage.

It could have been either instinct or some slight, barely detectable sound that made Ridge freeze and tense up. A feeling of immediate close danger flooded suddenly through him and instinctively he dropped into a crouch to prepare for the unknown.

That movement saved his life.

Tuned as his ears were to the slightest hint of sound around him, it seemed to Ridge that he heard the swish of the club rushing through the air even before it struck the rock above his head with a startling "crack."

Blindly he swung out with his left hand and heard a quiet groan as his fist struck the firm flesh of a stomach. But it was an ineffective blow and did not harm his attacker. Without warning, pain flashed through his left arm as the club descended on it.

Ridge tumbled forward, hoping to collide with the legs of his assailant and bring him down, but the man jumped quickly back and eluded him, thumping into the opposite wall. Ridge continued his roll and came up on his feet, blasting out with his pistol but striking nothing.

The club lashed out again and Ridge felt a bone snap in his right arm. His pistol went flying out of his hand.

"Damn you!" Parkman snarled as he

began to thrash the darkness with his left hand, kicking wildly and finally connecting a couple of times with his feet before the other man scrambled away to safety.

Ridge stood still for a moment, panting and tense, as his broken arm sent out shock waves of pain. He wished that he had not moved away from the place where his pistol had fallen. Now it would be impossible to locate it, and it was likely that his enemy was armed.

"I'm gonna kill you, Parkman," a bitter but slightly elated voice hissed from somewhere in the darkness. "I'm gonna split your skull open like a ripe watermelon."

"You ain't no ways near man enough to do that, Bramwell," Ridge said. "Without your gang of hired killers, you're like a rattler without no fangs."

As he spoke, Ridge began to move around, first a couple of steps to the right, then left, then back a few paces. When he thought he might have Bramwell at least partially confused about where he was, he paused and waited silently, his left hand reaching down and finding a stone about the size of his fist.

"Here's a fang for you," Bramwell snarled. The pistol shot cut a hole in the darkness like a bright yellow spear and the bullet went twanging away off the rock walls of the shaft. As the thunder of the report went rolling down the tunnel, some small rocks and dust dislodged from the ceiling, showering both men with gravel and choking dust.

Immediately Ridge hurled his rock, the throw a clumsy one because it came from his left hand. He heard the stone strike flesh, but Bramwell did not drop the pistol. He reached out for another rock, and, remarkably, his fingers touched the barrel of his lost pistol. Elatedly he picked it up.

He was hesitant to use the pistol now, though, because of the noise of the shots. The shock waves they caused could very easily bring the whole place down on top of them, and though he would have willingly given up his life if it meant Bramwell died too, he much preferred to kill Bramwell and live through it.

"I'll make a deal with you, Parkman," Bramwell said, his voice coming from some distance away. "You're between me an' my gold. If you'll strike a match an' hold up your hands, I'll tie you you up an' let you live."

"You go to hell, Bramwell," Ridge said.

Bramwell's pistol barked suddenly and the bullet struck uncomfortably near Ridge's head before ricocheting away. Ridge responded with a couple of shots of his own, and immediately portions of the roof began to tumble down.

Ignoring the impending danger of a cave-in, Bramwell was backing off toward the entrance of the mine, snapping off an occasional shot to keep Parkman back. Ridge knew he was in a desperate spot and began to quickly go over the options he had available to him.

He could stay there and let Bramwell get clear of the mine, then go after him once he had got out into the open. But once he got back to the area where DeWitt lay, Bramwell might very possibly kill the old man out of sheer meanness, or perhaps decide to chunk a stick or two of dynamite down toward Ridge, burying him forever under tons of rock.

He could go after Bramwell, but that would be a risky proposition, too. With his right arm broken, Ridge was having to shoot with his left hand, which had never been very accurate with a sidearm. And if he followed Bramwell on up the tunnel, it was possible that the outlaw might try to use DeWitt as a hostage to force Parkman to come out in the open and surrender.

He was literally damned if he did and damned if he didn't. Bramwell had two aces showing and Ridge was stuck trying to draw to an inside straight.

In the distance he heard Bramwell open the cylinder of his revolver and begin reloading. It was then or never, Ridge decided, rising to his feet and hurrying down the tunnel as quickly as his blind stumbling steps would permit him to go.

But he had only covered perhaps half the distance to Bramwell when the outlaw finished reloading and immediately fired three quick shots down the tunnel.

The cave-in began with a thick peppering of gravel and small stones. Then overburdened timbers began to crack and snap like toothpicks and tons of stone plummeted down into the mine with a deafening roar.

Ridge Parkman came to slowly. His first awareness was of pain. Next came the realization that, although his eyes were open, they saw nothing, and finally he remembered where he was.

With patient, almost casual, resignation, he began to analyze his condition. His right arm was throbbing violently — it was broken, he remembered. But there was a new sensation down lower, a heaviness on his feet and legs — rocks from the cave-in, he decided. He knew both legs were probably broken, but his stunned body had yet to send to his brain the signals of agony which the crushed bones and flesh would soon begin transmitting. Clouds of thick, invisible rock dust made breathing a nearly impossible chore.

He somehow knew that the cave-in had been centered up ahead of him toward the entrance. Bramwell was probably dead now, but if he was not, Ridge reflected, it would be a simple task for him to come back here and kill himself a deputy marshal. That would not do him much good now, though, since they both seemed to be trapped, and Ridge reflected that dying from a bullet might be much preferable to the slow death from suffocation and rotting wounds.

"Ridge?"

The voice was far away, muffled, insistent, and cautious.

"Ridge Parkman!"

Ridge considered it a moment and decided he might as well answer. He drew a breath, but the thick dust immediately clogged his windpipe, setting off a fit of violent coughing.

"I heard somethin'."

"Me too. Must be somebody's still alive back there. Come on."

The dust above Ridge began to take on a

faint glow which grew and intensified as he watched. There was the grating sound of footsteps on gravel and a voice said, "Don't disturb none of the rocks an' don't say nothin' loud, Abe. Anythin' we do might set it off again."

"Abe?" Ridge managed to call out.

"Yeh, Ridge," Abe's voice answered from somewhere. "Where you at, boy?"

"Here."

"Jes' keep talkin' an' I'll find you."

"Watch out for Bramwell. He's around here someplace if he ain't dead. My legs . . ."

Forms materialized in the fog above Ridge and stooped down over him. One carried a lamp and the other a lit candle.

"Let's see how bad it is 'fore we move 'im."

"No. First we get him the hell outa here an' then we check him."

Hands grabbed Parkman under his arms and pulled him slowly and carefully from under the pile of rock which covered his legs. Surprisingly, the pain which he expected to come was not nearly as intense as he had anticipated.

"Can you walk, son?"

"Dunno." He was hauled to his feet and amazingly his legs began to function, accepting the weight of his body. Abe and

DeWitt started half leading, half dragging him away.

"Not down that way," Ridge protested. "We've gotta get outa here."

"Where in tarnation you think we're takin' you? We're headin' out."

"But Bramwell —"

"Don't you pay no nevermind to Bramwell," DeWitt reassured him. "We didn't come acrost him on our way back here, an' if he was farther down that tunnel than you was, he's a gone hombre by now."

Ridge finally began to realize that sometime during the fight with Bramwell both of them had become disoriented. When Bramwell had made his flight toward what he thought was the outside and freedom, he had actually been working his way deeper into the dangerous portion of the mine, and Ridge, who had thought he was trapped by the cave-in, was actually on the safe side of the tons of fallen rock.

As Abe and DeWitt led him out of the mine, the sunlight sent sharp needles of pain into his eyes and forced him to clamp them tightly closed. The two men leaned him against a boulder and he just sat there a moment, drinking in the fresh air. Finally he opened his eyes slightly and they began to adjust to the light of day.

Down the hillside from the direction of town came the sound of approaching hoofbeats. Soon Oak and Lott came riding up, followed by Lieutenant Tinker and half a dozen of the cavalry men. As Lott leaped out of the saddle and rushed over to his deputy, Ridge began slowly rising to his feet, still astounded that his legs were intact and working.

"What in the hell happened here?" Lott demanded. "We heard the roar clear down in town."

"It was Bramwell," Ridge said. "Back in the mine there. He died in the cave-in."

"What was Bramwell doin' in there?" Lott asked. "He shoulda been long gone by now."

"He couldn't leave without the stolen gold," Ridge said. "I guess it's still in there, too, buried somewhere back under all that rock."

"You mean that skunk was hidin' all the gold he stole in my mine?" Mike DeWitt growled in surprise.

"It makes sense when you think about it," Ridge said. "An abandoned mine close to town that everybody knew wasn't safe. Even the location was perfect. All he had to do was look out the back window of the freight office to see if anybody was messin' around up here. He musta started sweatin' bullets when you came back up here an' set up shop again."

"Then he's the one that walloped me," DeWitt said. "Whacked me while I was still sleepin', I figger."

"Shore. He's probably been hidin' back in there ever since he got away from us after the shoot-out in town. He waited a few days until everybody figgered he was plumb outa the territory, then stole himself some transportation an' come back up here to get his booty."

Exhausted, Ridge sat back down on the ground and accepted the canteen which Oak offered him. It had been a rough time ever since he got here. A lot of men had died and his own escapes had all been entirely too close, but he felt good now. He could leave DeWitt's Strike knowing that at last all the loose ends were tied up and that Max Bramwell would never go on to victimize another mining camp in another place.

"Wal," DeWitt said, "it looks like now I've got me a whole shaft full of gold. Probably the richest mine in these here parts."

"Yeh," Abe agreed. "An' you won't have a bit of trouble findin' help to dig it out. There's a whole town full of miners down there that'll be just itchin' to lend a hand."